Danger in the Extreme

At five thousand feet, a safe skydiving altitude, Frank and Joe got ready to jump. Joe opened the door and looked out. "This is a pretty intense way to drop in for a visit," he said.

Frank laughed as he pulled down his goggles. "See you on the ground," he said, and jumped out into the wind.

Seconds later Joe followed. The wind grabbed him momentarily as he cleared the plane, then he was falling free and clear. He enjoyed the view as he counted off the seconds. Then he pulled his rip cord.

From experience, Joe expected the chute to jerk him up as it opened and caught air. He felt a slight tug, that was all. He heard a ripping sound and looked up. His heart caught in his throat.

His main chute and his reserve had come out in one big tangled ball. The wind whipped at the knotted mass over his head. He was not slowing down.

The Hardy Boys Mystery Stories

Available from MINSTREL Books

THE HARDY BOYS®

152

DANGER IN THE EXTREME

FRANKLIN W. DIXON

A MINSTREL® BOOK

Published by POCKET BOOKS

New York London Toronto Sydney Tokyo Singapore

A MINSTREL PAPERBACK *Original*

 A Minstrel Book published by
POCKET BOOKS, a division of Simon & Schuster Inc.
1230 Avenue of the Americas, New York, NY 10020

Copyright © 1998 by Simon & Schuster Inc.

Front cover illustration by John Youssi

Produced by Mega-Books, Inc.

ISBN: 0-671-02173-7

First Minstrel Books printing October 1998

10 9 8 7 6 5 4 3 2

THE HARDY BOYS MYSTERY STORIES is a trademark of Simon & Schuster Inc.

THE HARDY BOYS, A MINSTREL BOOK and colophon are registered trademarks of Simon & Schuster Inc.

Printed in the U.S.A.

Contents

1 Fear Drops In

"Come on, Frank!" Joe Hardy exclaimed, chucking his older brother on the shoulder. "This is it—the Max Games! Get pumped."

Frank smiled as he tugged his ski cap down over his brown hair. He, Joe, and their friend Jamal Hawkins stood in the parking lot of the Bayport University football stadium. A hundred or so other people jostled around them.

Frank glanced up. The stadium lights blazed bright yellow against the dark sky. Hard rock blared from the speakers. "I'm psyched," he replied calmly.

Jamal laughed. "Are you sure you're into this, Frank? Maybe you should be playing chess and sipping hot tea instead of sky surfing."

"Wait till you see how excited I get when I humble you on the ice wall," Frank said.

At about five feet ten, Jamal was a few inches shorter than Frank, but he was an excellent athlete and never backed down from a challenge. He nodded at Frank. "Bring it on, tall man," he said. "We'll see if you can back up that big talk."

A television news crew came up to the teens. "Excuse me," a reporter said. "Did you say you were entered in the sky-surfing competition?"

When Frank nodded, the reporter snapped her fingers at the cameraman, who lifted the camera to his shoulder and aimed it at Frank. "We're rolling," he said.

Quickly the reporter got the three friends' names. She turned back to the camera and switched on her microphone. "I'm here in Bayport at the third annual Max Games, the Olympics of extreme sports," she said. "This weekend star athletes from around the world will compete in events such as snowboard aerials, downhill mountain bike racing, and speed ice climbing. Danger is the name of the game here at the Max Games."

The reporter faced Frank. "Frank," she asked, "what events are you three entered in?"

Frank looked into the camera and blushed. "Ah, Jamal and I are in the ice-climbing event and—"

"Tell us about that."

"Well," Frank said, "you've got a fifty-foot-high

wall of ice, and the object is to free climb to the top as fast as you can."

"Free climb?"

"No ropes," Jamal interrupted. "You have a safety harness, but you can't use ropes to climb, only ice axes."

The reporter smiled at the camera. "Doesn't sound like an event for someone afraid of heights."

"It's only dangerous if you fall," Jamal said. "Otherwise, it's perfectly safe."

The reporter laughed and then turned to Joe. "How about you?"

"I'm racing in the snocross."

"That's where souped-up snowmobiles fly around in a big circle, right?"

Joe shrugged. "I guess that about sums it up."

"And what about the sky surfing. I know everyone at home wants to hear about that."

"Sure," Joe said. "All three of us are entered in that event. My brother, Frank, here jumps out of a plane at ten thousand feet. He rides a sky ski and . . ."

The reporter wrinkled her brow. "A sky ski?"

"It's like a snowboard or a water ski," Frank said.

"Exactly," Joe continued. "While he free-falls he does all kinds of stunts. You know, flips, spins, dives."

"And what do you do?"

"I'll be wearing a helmet camera," Joe said. "I'll

fall with him, filming the stunts so the judges can see them."

"You guys are insane," the reporter teased. "Who flies the plane? That's the job I would want."

"Jamal is our pilot," Joe said. "He flies for his dad's air taxi service."

"Jamal, you sound like the smart one to me. Thanks, guys." The reporter faced the camera again. "Well, there you have it. Three Max Games contestants ready to climb walls and jump out of planes just for the chance at a medal."

"Okay. It's time for the opening ceremony!" a loud voice called.

Max Games officials, dressed in metallic silver parkas, herded the news crew away and spoke to the athletes: "Go through the gate, around the track, and then sit in the bleachers at the far end of the stadium. Got it?"

"Not very organized," Frank muttered, remembering the way Olympic athletes marched into a stadium in perfect columns carrying their countries' flags.

The crowd moved forward slowly. Joe grinned as he watched the group in front of him. "Those guys have more logos pasted on them than race cars."

"Yeah," Jamal said, pointing to an athlete whose ski jacket was covered with colorful patches with the names of soft drinks, snowboard equipment, and car makers. "That guy's a walking advertisement."

"Landing a sponsor," Joe said wistfully, "would be great. I'd love to have someone give me an awesome snowmobile and hire me to race all over the country."

"Keep on dreaming," Frank said as they passed through the gate and into the stadium.

"Right," Jamal quipped. "That's the only place you're going to get a medal—in your dreams."

Before Joe could reply, a huge roar went up from the crowd.

"Wow!" Joe said. "There must be twenty thousand people here."

The athletes waved up at the cheering crowd.

A television camera followed them along the running track that circled the stadium.

"Looks like we're on TV again," Jamal said, shouting over the crowd and music. "Wave to everyone at home."

The athletes walked slowly past the stands. To their left was the football field, which had been transformed into a snocross course.

Like a motocross rider jumping his dirt bike over mountains of earth, Joe would soon be racing his snowmobile over mounds of snow piled three stories high. Between the big jumps the course was a rugged series of ruts, banked hairpin turns, and bone-jarring whoop-de-doos. Hay bales were stacked all along the course to stop or slow down runaway snowmobiles in order to minimize the impact of crashes.

Just after the athletes climbed into the bleachers and sat down, the stadium lights shut down and the speakers went silent. The crowd murmured in nervous anticipation.

A few seconds later an explosion ripped through the darkness. Frank jumped. He looked up into the sky as a huge purple starburst opened up high over the stadium. Flickering embers shimmered above the crowd like radioactive raindrops for a second or two, then flamed out.

"Fireworks," Joe said. "Excellent."

Rockets exploded from tubes along the base of the stands. They shot high overhead, then burst into multicolored spheres that seemed as large as planets.

The show continued for more than ten minutes. Then, just as quickly as it had begun, it was over. The stadium was dark again, and the smell of cordite and black powder hung in the cold air.

"I wonder what's next," Joe whispered.

"There!" Jamal said, pointing at the upper lip of the stadium.

Laser strobe lights beamed down over the crowd from both sides of the stadium. The crowd gasped as red, yellow, and green lights played off the fresh snow on the race course.

Finally all the lights focused on a stagelike platform across the field, under the scoreboard.

A big man dressed in a silver parka appeared on

6

the platform, a microphone in his hand. He nodded to someone on the ground and an enormous Jumbotron video monitor came on behind him. When he saw himself magnified to forty feet tall on the screen, he raised his hands over his head and called to the crowd: "I'm Fred Vale. Welcome to the third annual Max Games!"

The crowd roared in approval.

Vale wore wraparound mirrored sunglasses and a bristly dark goatee.

"Pretty intense," Jamal said. "Mirrored shades at night."

"Yeah," Joe agreed. "Dude looks like a pro wrestler or something."

Vale waited for the cheers to die down, then continued. "Our motto here is: If you don't get hurt, you didn't try hard enough!"

This time all the athletes jumped up and cheered.

Smiling broadly, Fred Vale motioned with his hands for everyone to sit back down.

"Thank you," he said. "I can tell you all have the right attitude. This is going to be the best Max Games yet!"

The music kicked in again, though not so loud now. The crowd could easily hear Vale's booming voice over it.

"Now, to kick off the games I'd like to direct your attention to the Jumbotron," Vale shouted.

"Watch as two-time defending sky-surfing champions Sammy Fear and Amanda Mollica demonstrate this death-defying sport."

Frank craned his neck to look up overhead. He couldn't see anything but stars in the night sky.

He heard a murmur from the crowd and looked at the Jumbotron. Vale's image had disappeared, replaced by fuzzy static. A jumpy picture flickered on and off for a few seconds, then became clear.

"It's Bayport," someone said.

Sure enough, Frank recognized the lights of downtown Bayport and the dark horizon as it would be seen from someone thousands of feet in the air. In the corner of the picture was the strut and part of the wing of an airplane. The picture rotated back into the plane. It focused on a lean young man in a white jumpsuit. He had long blond hair and wore tinted goggles.

"It's Sammy Fear," Frank said. Amanda Mollica's helmet cam was obviously on and working fine.

The crowd gasped as the camera watched Fear jump from the plane. Mollica followed. The picture went black, then focused squarely on Sammy Fear. He plummeted through the air in a standing position, arms outstretched from his sides like an old-time wave surfer hanging five. Sammy totally filled the huge Jumbotron screen.

"They must be only three or four feet apart," Frank commented.

"They're good," Joe agreed.

With just the slightest movement of his left hand, Fear went into a superfast spin. Then just as quickly as he'd started, he halted and flipped over so he was diving headfirst toward the earth.

Joe looked up. He thought he could make out Fear's white jumpsuit against the darkness now. He knew that Fear and Mollica had about forty-five seconds of free-fall before they would have to pull their chutes.

"Cool!" someone behind them shouted.

Fear now performed a quick series of five back-flips followed by some full layout front-twisting somersaults. He then froze in a standing position again.

"Now it's Mollica's turn to show off," Jamal said.

He was right. Suddenly the picture of Fear flipped over so it looked as if he was going down headfirst, but the sky and stars were still over his head. Mollica was now filming him from upside down.

Somehow she made herself swing around Fear in a series of full circles, filming him from every angle.

"Nice!" Joe said. "Their timing is perfect."

Frank had a concerned look on his face. "Their timing's going to be way off if they don't pull out soon. Look."

Joe looked up in the sky. The two surfers were clearly visible now, and falling at a fast one hundred twenty miles per hour.

People in the crowd noticed them at the same

time and started pointing up in the sky and calling out nervously.

"They're just showing off," Jamal said.

"They'd be disqualified in a competition," Frank said. "The rules say you've got to pull at a safe altitude."

The Jumbotron showed Fear blithely falling in a seated position now, his hands clasped behind his head as if he were relaxing in front of a TV.

Shouts started going up from the crowd. The music cut off. Fear and Mollica kept falling.

The Jumbotron went black.

"Oh, man," Jamal said. "I don't want to see them splat."

A cheer went up from the crowd as a bright orange chute bloomed above the smaller of the two figures.

"Mollica pulled her chute," Frank said.

Fear kept falling, his arms and legs held out as if he were about to belly flop into a pool.

"Something must be wrong!" Frank shouted. "His chute's not opening!"

A girl close by covered her eyes and let out a frightened sob.

Sammy Fear was headed straight for the center of the stadium.

2 Assignment: Secret Service

While twenty thousand people watched, Fear's body abruptly jerked up like a puppet whose strings had just been yanked.

"His chute's out," Frank said. "But he's still going too fast!"

An oversize rectangular-shape parachute unfolded above the sky surfer. The force wrenched him sideways into a spiral. He was now only a couple of hundred feet over the stadium, falling like a bird with a wounded wing.

"He's headed toward the upper deck," Joe said, pointing. "He's going to land right on the crowd."

The athletes watched as hundreds of spectators jumped to their feet and started scrambling over one another to get out of their seats.

At a height barely higher than the tops of the stadium light poles, Sammy Fear pulled down hard on the brake toggles of his chute.

Lifting his feet up like those of a long jumper reaching for extra distance, he swooped down over the panicked crowd. His feet barely missing people's heads, he arced along the upper decks, then swung down smoothly over the center of the field. Dropping his feet, he landed at a jog neatly on top of one of the snocross jumps. He pulled the releases, and his chute billowed away from him in the breeze.

"Wow!" was all Frank could say.

The crowd was silent for a second or two, then everyone erupted into wild cheers. The other Max Games athletes were on their feet clapping.

"Here comes Mollica," Joe said as Fear's partner drifted in and landed softly next to him.

The stadium lights snapped back on. The Jumbotron picture came back up, showing the two sky surfers standing next to each other.

Mollica and Fear seemed to exchange a few words.

"Looks like she's mad at him," Frank said. "She must not have known he was going to pull that stunt."

As Mollica and Fear took their bows and gathered up their chutes, Fred Vale came back on, breathless and relieved. He led the crowd in a final ovation.

"I hope you'll come to as many events as you can this weekend," he continued. "The Max Games are always this exciting!"

"I sure hope not," Jamal said with a wry grin. "I don't think I could take it."

"Stay in your seats, everyone," Vale continued. "The preliminary heats of the snocross are coming right up."

Joe started down the bleachers. "That's me."

He, Frank, and Jamal stepped out of the stands along with the other athletes who had to prepare for events.

As Fear and Mollica came walking over, a voice from high in the stands shouted down: "Hey, Fear! You're dangerous—you take too many chances!"

Fear raised his fist, punching the air. "That's why I'm the best there is, man!"

Mollica put her hand on his shoulder, obviously upset by his crazy antics.

Before the confrontation could get out of control, Max Games officials rushed in and whisked the two sky surfers away.

"I have to agree with whoever that was," Frank said. "If Fear's chute hadn't opened perfectly, he'd be dead."

"And a lot of people in the stands would have been hurt," Jamal added.

"Yeah, but you've got to admit he knew how to make a good show," Joe said.

Jamal shrugged, turning up the collar of his

13

leather flight jacket. "The Max Games TV ratings will skyrocket after tonight, if that's what you mean. I'm going to check out the climbing wall. You want to go, Frank?"

"Not yet," Frank replied. "After Joe's heat I might be over."

Jamal wished Joe good luck and took off. The Hardys headed around the snocross track toward a wide tunnel that led under the stadium stands. As they reached the mouth of the tunnel, a woman in a dark suit and coat approached them. She stepped in front of Joe and held up an official-looking ID.

"Joe Hardy?" she asked.

Joe stopped in his tracks. "Yeah."

"My name is Michelle DuBelle. I'm with the Secret Service. Can I talk to you and your brother for a moment?"

Joe glanced at Frank. "Sure," he said. "What's going on?"

DuBelle pocketed her ID and led the Hardys a few yards away from the athletes milling around the mouth of the entrance tunnel.

DuBelle shot a glance back over her right shoulder. "You know who that is?"

The Hardys followed the agent's gaze about thirty yards down the running track. Frank spotted a sullen-looking kid about sixteen years old standing next to the wall leading up into the stands. He wore a bulky green army surplus jacket, baggy jeans, heavy black boots, and a baseball cap on

14

backward. Two square-shouldered men in dark overcoats stood next to him.

"Hey, isn't that . . . no," Frank said doubtfully.

"Yes, it is," DuBelle said. "That's Neal Jordan, the son of the president of the United States."

"Excellent," Joe said. "He's here to watch?"

"No, he's here to compete," DuBelle said. "Even though we advised against it, he's going to be in the snowboard aerials."

Joe frowned. He'd never seen Jordan at any previous contests. He wondered how Neal had qualified for the Max Games.

DuBelle answered his question for him.

"Neal called Fred Vale behind his father's back, and of course Vale said he could compete. I'm sure Vale figures having Neal here will help the games get extra attention. We've been fighting off his cameras all night."

"Why tell us all this?" Frank asked. He noticed Jordan looking over at them.

"I met your father in Washington last year," DuBelle replied. "He told me about you two, and I decided to ask you if you'd be willing to help us keep an eye on Neal during our stay in Bayport."

The Hardys looked at each other. Their father, Fenton Hardy, was a well-known private detective who often helped government agencies with their investigations. Still, Frank couldn't believe they were being given such an incredible responsibility—to guard the president's son!

15

"Sure," Frank and Joe said in unison.

DuBelle smiled. "Great. Listen, Neal's a good kid, but he hates having us crowding around him all the time. Sometimes he even tries to sneak away."

Joe crossed his arms in front of his chest. "Doesn't he understand someone might try to kidnap him or something?"

"I think so, but he wants to feel like a normal teenager. He's seen you guys compete, and I think he'd really like to hang out with you, if you're okay with that."

One of the other agents came striding over, his hands jammed in his coat pockets. "Michelle, I have to tell you again—this is a bad idea."

"Frank and Joe Hardy, meet Agent Kenneth Ardis."

Frank held out a hand to shake Ardis's, but the agent ignored him.

"These two kids can't protect Neal," he said to DuBelle. "And having them around may cause other agents to relax instead of doing their jobs the way they should."

"It's my call," DuBelle said sternly. "Get back to your post."

Ardis glared at the Hardys, his teeth clenched. He turned and marched back to his station a few yards away from Neal.

"Come on," DuBelle said, smiling. "Let me introduce you."

DuBelle led the Hardys over to Neal, dropping

16

back just before they reached him to give the teens room. "Neal," she said. "This is Frank and Joe Hardy."

Neal leaned forward a little and pulled one hand out of his pocket. He held out a clenched fist.

Joe knocked his fist against Neal's. Frank did the same, then Neal's hand disappeared back into his jacket. "So, you two got drafted to be my friends?"

Frank smiled. "No, we volunteered. You aren't going to make us sorry, are you?"

Neal just shrugged. "Hey," he said, nodding at Joe. "You in the snocross?"

"Yeah," Joe replied. "Actually, I've got to get ready now. You gonna watch?"

"'Course," Neal said. "Rage, man. Get out there and tear it up."

"Just watch," Joe said. "Later."

After his brother disappeared under the stands to change and get his snowmobile, Frank tried to talk to Neal. He could feel the Secret Service agents watching them. He counted four agents in suits and figured a few more were close by, dressed as spectators.

"So, you're in the snowboard aerials?"

Neal nodded slightly but said nothing.

This is going to be difficult, Frank thought. He decided to be patient and say nothing. Neal would open up soon.

They stood leaning against the side wall of the stadium. They watched Max Games workers with rakes and shovels make final preparations to the snocross course. They watched spectators come down out of the stands and head under the stadium to the snack bar. Every once in a while someone would pause and stare at Neal as if he recognized him. A couple of teenage girls giggled and pointed in their direction.

Finally Neal said something. "This music is lame."

Frank listened to the rock coming out of the stadium speakers. "It is pretty tired," he agreed. "You'd think the Max Games would be more on the edge."

Neal nodded. "Speed metal or industrial. I asked them to play some Tragic Hayride when I pop my aerials. They looked at me like I was some kind of space alien."

"That's a good band," Frank said. "You think country punk goes well with your jumps."

Neal seemed impressed that Frank had heard of Tragic Hayride. "It gets me in the right mood," he said.

At that moment the music from the speakers died down and an announcer came on. "Max Games ushers, please clear the track for the snocross."

Max Games employees working on the snocross course stopped immediately and jumped over the hay bales and onto the running track. Other employees guided stray spectators back to the stands.

Ken Ardis and Michelle DuBelle motioned for

Frank and Neal to get off the track. Neal reluctantly led the way to a couple of prime front-row seats. Frank noticed that the young couple in the ski parkas sitting right next to them wore what looked like tiny hearing aids. He realized they, too, must be Secret Service. He could understand how Neal felt—constantly watched, like an exotic insect caught in a jar.

"Where's your family?" Frank asked. "Are they going to watch you compete?"

Neal shook his head. "Having Dad here would cause too much of an uproar, even for that Vale character."

The woman in the parka next to Neal shot him a quick glance, then looked away.

Neal leaned close to Frank and whispered, "I'm not supposed to tell anyone where my dad is, but I'll tell you. My family's at our vacation home up in the Catskill Mountains. It's just a short plane ride from here, and I'm going there after the games."

A motorized cart with a twenty-five-foot boom attached to it trundled by in front of Neal and Frank. A network television camera panned back and forth, scanning the track, then turned back on them. Neal flipped his cap around and pulled it down over his eyes.

The camera darted away as a crescendo of noise rose from under the stands. A few seconds later ten brightly colored, souped-up snowmobiles came rumbling out. The drivers, dressed in riding suits and helmets, guided their machines through a break in the hay bales and up to the starting line of the snocross. The crowd cheered loudly.

"Which one's Joe?" Neal asked.

"There," Frank said, pointing to a muscular figure on a dark blue snowmobile. "He's in the blue suit and helmet—number eight."

With the competitors lined up perfectly, the starter dropped the flag.

Ten engines revved in unison, spraying back huge rooster tails of wet snow. Riders kicked at one another and jostled for position going into the first sharp turn.

"I can't see Joe," Frank said. "Where is he?"

Neal and Frank watched the row of snowmobiles turn into a single-file line as they tore through the first turn and then ramped up over the first jump. The four-hundred-pound machines crashed back to earth with a tremendous *whump!*

"There he is!" Neal shouted. "He's out in front."

They watched Joe's snowmobile buck over the whoop-de-doos like a bronco. A rider in a fluorescent green race suit was right next to him fighting for the lead.

"That's Jim 'Justice' Edwards!" Neal shouted over the noise. "If you do something to him, he comes back at you twice as hard. He's a total maniac."

Joe maintained the lead coming around the far turn. As the racers moved up to complete the first lap, Edwards tried to scoot by Joe for an inside pass, but Joe cut him off.

"That's it, Joe!" Frank shouted. "Don't let him by."

Joe rocketed up the big jump with Edwards right on his tail. They both went airborne at the same time. The two seemed to hover in midair together, fifteen feet above the track.

Frank's heart skipped a beat as he suddenly realized what was going to happen.

Jim Edwards flew just a little bit farther than Joe. Joe landed. A split second later Edwards came down right on top of him.

The two snowmobiles came together with a sickening crunch. The crowd gasped.

Edwards bounced off Joe, hit the ground, and veered ahead, staying in control.

Joe wasn't so lucky. He flew off his snowmobile and tumbled into the hay bales. His helmet came off and bounced across the running track. When Joe finally came to a stop, he lay there, legs bent at awkward angles, motionless.

3 Missing

Officials waved their red flags frantically, trying to stop the race before someone ran over Joe.

Frank and Neal leaped from their seats. The agent next to Neal tried to reach out to stop him, but the president's son wrenched himself free. He and Frank rushed to the track.

Fred Vale and an official with a medical kit were already kneeling by Joe's side when Frank got there. The other racers had all stopped, and the stadium was silent as the crowd waited to find out Joe's condition.

Vale had his sunglasses hanging around his neck on a lanyard. "What's your name? Joe Hardy? Okay, Joe, are you hurt?" he asked. "Can you move your legs?"

A cameraman hovered nearby, shifting around for the best angle.

Frank pushed the medic aside and crouched by his brother.

"Frank?" Joe said weakly.

"It's me, Joe. How do you feel?"

Joe shook his head, then straightened his legs into a more comfortable position. "I think I'm okay. Got the wind knocked out of me, that's for sure."

"That was a gnarly wipeout," Neal said, helping Frank lift Joe to a seated position.

Vale stood up. "You're not hurt? Not even a broken arm or something?" He seemed almost disappointed.

"No, I'm fine. How's my snowmobile?" Joe stood up, and the crowd cheered when they saw he wasn't hurt.

Vale grinned and put his shades back on. "That's the spirit." He turned to the cameraman. "Did you get the crash?"

The man nodded.

"Awesome!" Vale clapped his hands together. "Here, get Neal Jordan in the picture helping his friend Joe. And get these Secret Service agents, too."

Ken Ardis went over and covered the lens with his hand. "That's enough," he said.

"Okay, okay," Vale said, holding his hands up. "I got what I needed. Come on," he said to the cameraman. "I want to get that tape to the local news so they can show it later tonight. It'll really bring in the crowds tomorrow."

Agent DuBelle took Neal by the arm. "Let's go," she ordered. "Joe's okay. Back to the stands."

Another race official came over and handed Joe his helmet. "You sure you're okay, young man?"

Joe nodded.

"Well," the official continued, "nobody even completed the first lap. So if you're up for it, we're going to restart the race in"—he glanced at his watch—"three minutes."

"If my ride's okay, I'll be there," Joe said.

The Hardys walked over to Joe's snowmobile. It lay on its side next to the hay bales. Frank and the official helped Joe roll it upright.

"The handlebars are a little bent," Frank noted.

Joe steered left and right. "As long as it runs." He turned the key and punched the ignition switch. The supertuned engine fired to life.

Joe got on his snowmobile and put on his helmet. He strapped it on extra tight this time; he didn't want the thing flying off again. He gave his brother a high five. "All I have to do is finish in the top four," he said. "Wish me luck."

Joe gunned the engine, and the rubber tanklike track bit into the snow and launched the snowmobile forward. He headed back to the starting line.

Frank joined Neal in the stands.

"He's going to try to race again?" Neal asked in disbelief.

Frank nodded. "Joe's pretty stubborn."

"Nice," Neal said. "I think I'm going to like you guys."

The race started again. This time Jim Edwards easily pulled out in front.

"He's all alone," Neal said. "No one's even challenging him."

Frank held his breath. He could tell Joe was struggling to keep his snowmobile under control. "Joe'll be lucky to make it through this heat," he said.

It became a race for second, third, and fourth. The crowd cheered every time Joe successfully landed a jump. The front end of his snowmobile shook and jumped as he bounded over the whoop-de-doos.

Every time he made the turn at the far end of the track, Frank lost sight of him. Then he would see the dark blue snowmobile pop up into the air as Joe attacked the jumps on the far side of the track.

Several racers smashed into one another going around a turn.

"Watch it, Joe!" Frank shouted.

Joe threw his weight to the left, barely dodging the accident.

Up ahead Jim Edwards launched his snowmobile high into the air off the last jump. In midair he stood up and let go of the handlebars, playing to the crowd as he crossed the finish line.

"Wow!" Neal shouted. "Fat stalled air!"

A few seconds later Joe wrestled his damaged ride under the checkered flag to the finish line in third place—good enough to qualify for the next round.

Frank sighed with relief.

When he and Neal left the stands to congratulate Joe, Agent DuBelle intercepted them. "Time to go, Neal," she said.

Neal's shoulders sagged, but he didn't argue.

"Hey," Frank said. "I'm going to practice on the ice wall tomorrow morning. Want to come?"

Neal looked at Agent DuBelle. She nodded her assent. "Be in the Metropolitan Hotel lobby at eight," she said to Frank. "The two of you can drive over together."

Neal smiled and held out his fist to Frank again. "Later," he said. "Tell your brother 'Righteous race.'"

As agents whisked Neal away, Frank went to look for Joe. He found his brother under the stadium, where all the riders had separate pit areas set up to work on their snowmobiles.

Joe had thrown his helmet and gloves to the cement floor. He had a wrench in his hand and was busy loosening the right ski.

"Nice work," Frank said.

"Thanks, bro." Joe stood up and dropped the

wrench in disgust. "My steering's shot, though. I'll never make it through the next round tomorrow unless I get this thing fixed." He turned to his brother. "It was Edwards who ran over me, wasn't it?"

Frank nodded. "It looked like he did it intentionally."

A female voice interrupted them. "He did."

The Hardys turned to see a young woman about their own age. She had long, dark hair and wore a white jumpsuit.

"Hey, Amanda," Frank said. He knew Sammy Fear's sky-surfing partner from previous competitions. "You saw Joe's wipeout?"

She laughed. "See it? I couldn't believe he walked away from it." She looked at Joe. "You sure you're okay?"

"Better than my racer," Joe said, giving his snowmobile a kick. "I'd like to give Jim Edwards a little tune-up, though. Only problem is, I don't see him around anywhere."

"He's in a stall around the corner," Amanda said, pointing down the wide hall behind the Hardys. "I think your head did some damage to his snowmobile."

Joe started down the hall, but Frank grabbed him by the shoulder. "Save it for the track, Joe. You don't want to get disqualified."

"Yeah, Joe," Amanda said. "You've just got to

understand how desperate Edwards is. Remember when he got injured last year?"

Joe nodded.

"His sponsors dropped him," she continued. "He's paying his own way this year, and he really needs the prize money."

"Enough to take my brother's head off?" Frank asked.

"Like I said, he's desperate. He'll do just about anything to win."

Joe started putting his tools away. "He's always been dangerous. We trade knocks every race, but this is the first time he's tried to take me out like that."

Amanda pursed her lips and nodded sympathetically. "Yeah. He definitely wants you out of the way."

"What about you?" Frank teased. "That was some chance you and Sammy took tonight. I thought for a second his chute had malfunctioned."

"Believe me, I had no idea Sammy was going to pull that stupid stunt," Amanda said, shaking her finger in the air. "I was just as scared as you guys were."

"Fred Vale seemed to like it," Joe said, digging in his tool box for a socket wrench. "He's out for blood."

"Yeah," Frank agreed. "He seemed pretty disappointed when you weren't hurt, Joe."

Amanda glanced around as if to see if anyone was listening. "I hear he has money problems," she whispered.

Frank's eyebrows went up. "Oh? I thought the Max Games made tons of money."

"They do," Amanda said. "Or they will this year, that is. He lost money on the first two Max Games because they weren't popular yet. And he dropped a whole lot of money on that rock concert last year."

"I remember that," Joe said. "The lead singer got sick, and Vale had to refund millions of dollars in tickets."

Amanda nodded. "If he doesn't get great TV ratings this year, there may be no Max Games next year."

Frank gave his brother a playful shove. "So there," he said. "You should thank Jim Edwards for flattening you. You guys are helping to keep ratings high."

Joe slapped the socket wrench against the palm of his hand. "I'll give Vale something to see next time I run into Edwards."

Amanda smiled. "I just wanted to make sure you were okay," she said, turning to go. "On the other hand, if you get too caught up with snocross, you might as well give the sky-surfing gold medal to Sammy and me."

"No way," Frank said. "That medal's ours." He waved goodbye.

After Amanda was gone, Frank helped Joe lock up his tools and cover his snowmobile.

With everything secure, they made their way back out onto the field. The crowd was cheering the final preliminary heat of the snocross, but Joe was in no mood to watch.

"Let's just go home," he said. "I'm tired."

The brothers skirted the track and headed back out the main entrance to the parking lot.

The lot seemed dark after the bright lights of the stadium. The Hardys' van was parked somewhere in the middle, but Frank stopped about halfway there.

"What's up?" Joe asked.

Frank pointed to a pair of steel doors about fifty yards from the main stadium entrance. A security light glowed over the doors, and a shiny black sport utility vehicle with tinted windows was idling right in front of them.

"That must be Neal Jordan's motorcade," Joe said. "I bet they take him in and out through that private entrance."

Now Frank spotted another black truck parked behind the sport-ute. Five Bayport police cruisers were spaced evenly along the drive leading to the main road.

A police radio squawked, but no one picked up the call.

"What are they doing?" Frank asked. "I figured they'd be long gone by now."

"Something's wrong," Joe agreed. "No one's guarding that truck. And where are all the cops who go with those cruisers?"

The Hardys heard footsteps moving toward them in the darkness. Frank spun around.

It was Agent DuBelle, her face pale.

"Frank! Joe!" she said, gasping for breath. "Have you seen Neal? He's disappeared."

4 Snocross Double Cross

"How did it happen?" Joe asked.

"We had him at that entrance," DuBelle said, pointing to the steel doors. "Agent Ardis drove the truck around—" Her walkie-talkie crackled to life. She pulled it from her belt. "Agent One," she said.

"We have officers stationed at the back entrance and sweeping the stands," a male voice said. "Nothing so far."

"Nothing at the front," DuBelle said. "Continue the sweep. Out." She looked at Frank. "He just took off. We lost him in a stairwell."

Frank thought for a moment, then started to run back into the stadium. "I have an idea," he said. Joe and DuBelle followed him at a fast jog.

Frank retraced the path he and Joe had just

walked, ending up under the stadium next to Joe's snowmobile. Snocross drivers from the last heat were busy parking their machines and talking over the race. Frank slowed to a walk.

"What would he be doing down here?" Joe asked.

Frank held up a hand as if to say, "Just wait a second." He pushed between a pair of drivers and rounded the corner.

He stopped and pointed. "There he is."

Neal was standing next to Jim Edwards's bright green sled, talking to two other young men—Edwards and Sammy Fear.

Agent DuBelle was on her radio immediately. "Agent One to Agent Six," she said. "The egg is safe. I'm in . . . ah, sector sub-nine, I believe. Out." She sighed. "That kid drives me crazy. Frank, good call. If you guys could pry Neal away from his new friends, I'll work on securing the area."

The Hardys both nodded and went over to Jim Edwards's pit area.

While Sammy Fear was tall and thin, with long hair, Jim Edwards was about five feet ten and muscular, like a running back. His buzz-cut hair was dyed bright orange, and he'd shaved the word *Justice* across the back of his head.

Joe set his jaw to try to control his anger upon seeing Edwards. "Nice hair, Jim," he said, between clenched teeth.

Edwards spun around quickly. "Yo! Joe Hardy,"

he said with a grin. "Listen, man. I'm really sorry about the heat earlier."

"Yeah," Neal added. "Jim says it was an accident."

"I'm supposed to believe that?" Joe said, getting in Jim's face.

Sammy Fear stepped between them. "Whoa, keep the peace, fellows. It's over and nobody got hurt, right? Let's not get all hostile here in front of the president's son, eh?"

Joe held his ground. It was Edwards who took a step back, holding his hands up. "Joe, man. You gotta believe me. I ride hard. Trying to win, that's all."

Frank turned the attention back to Neal. "I guess you're a fan of 'Justice' Edwards, huh?"

Neal nodded enthusiastically. "Both these dudes, man." He held up a Max Games T-shirt. "Check it out, Frank. They both signed it."

"The young prez here tells me he's in the snowboard competition," Fear said. "That's sweet, man. I'll definitely be there to watch."

Neal blushed, obviously flattered.

"All right," Agent DuBelle said, stepping in. "Time to go."

Agent Ardis showed up and bumped into Frank as he and DuBelle led Neal away. "I told you having those boys watch Neal would only cause problems," he said, loud enough for the Hardys to hear.

The athletes watched as several agents cleared the way in front of the president's son.

"Ardis doesn't like us too much," Frank said after they'd gone.

"I guess those agents have a tough job," Edwards said. "You can't blame them for being rude to people." He held out his right hand to Joe. "No hard feelings?"

Reluctantly, Joe shook the hand. "See you on the track tomorrow," he said.

At home Fenton and Laura Hardy sat at the kitchen table, listening to their sons recount their exciting evening.

"I've never met Ken Ardis," Fenton was saying. "But I remember Agent DuBelle. She seemed very professional."

Frank laughed. "She has her work cut out for her."

"I'll say," Joe added. "Neal Jordan is a better escape artist than Houdini."

Laura Hardy brought more hot soup over from the stove and filled Joe's bowl. "I'm sure it's hard for Neal," she said. "All this attention every place he goes."

Joe slurped up a spoonful of vegetable soup. "I'm just psyched Agent DuBelle asked us to help. And then Frank here came to the rescue when he poofed. That was amazing. How'd you know he'd be talking to Jim?"

"A hunch," Frank said. "Neal doesn't say much, but while we were watching the snocross he seemed to be a big fan of Edwards."

Joe tipped the bowl and spooned up the rest of his soup. "Well," he said, wiping his mouth, "he's going to be disappointed when I whip up on Edwards in the final, then."

The Hardys all went into the living room to watch the late news. There, in the sports wrap-up, was a section on the Max Games. Sammy Fear was shown landing in the middle of the stadium, and then the footage cut to Edwards's landing his snowmobile right on top of Joe.

"If you can believe it," the sportscaster said, "the young man on the bottom, Joe Hardy, was not injured in the crack-up. He later returned to qualify for tomorrow's snocross semifinals."

Frank gave Joe a high five. "Excellent, man. You got your name on the sports highlights."

Laura Hardy gasped. "Goodness, Fenton," she said. "I don't know why we let the boys participate in such things."

"Because if we didn't, they'd be here all day tearing up the house," Fenton said with a grin.

After the news Frank and Joe said good night to their parents and headed upstairs to bed. The next morning, Saturday, was the first big day of competition.

* * *

It was seven o'clock, and the sun was barely up when the Hardys rolled out of bed and dragged themselves out to their van.

"Hold up," Joe said, running back into the house.

Frank could see his breath as he started the van and cranked up the heater. Joe returned a few minutes later, arms loaded with gear. He opened the sliding side door and dumped in two packed parachutes and the rest of their sky-surfing stuff.

"Sky surfing's not until tomorrow," Frank said.

Joe slammed the sliding door shut and climbed into the passenger seat. "I know," he said, tossing Frank a chocolate breakfast bar. "I just want to have everything in one place so we don't forget it."

Frank drove to the Metropolitan Hotel in downtown Bayport to meet Neal. The old building had a drive leading under an awning at the front door. Usually, several cars and taxicabs idled under the awning as guests checked in or out. This morning, however, a Bayport police officer stood at the door waving people on.

When Frank rolled in and stopped, the officer stepped quickly over to the driver's window. "You can't stop here," he said as Frank grabbed his climbing pack and hopped out. Joe slid into the driver's seat.

"Just getting dropped off, sir," Frank said politely.

The cop frowned. "Go on," he said to Joe. "Get this thing away from the door."

"See you at the games," Joe said, closing the door and taking off.

Frank noticed that all the parking meters along the street in front of the hotel were covered with orange No Parking signs. He figured the Secret Service must be worried about car bombs or something.

"What's in the bag?" the cop asked.

"Oh," Frank said, taking the pack from his shoulder. "My climbing gear."

The cop grabbed the pack and opened it. He pulled out an ice ax. "Hey, buddy. What's this?"

DuBelle and an agent Frank recognized from the night before stepped out of the hotel. "It's okay," DuBelle said. "He's been cleared."

The officer zipped the bag up and handed it back to Frank.

Inside, as Frank and DuBelle exchanged good mornings, Frank watched an agent exit from an elevator across the lobby. The man made a small hand signal to DuBelle, then spoke briefly into his radio.

A minute or so later, Neal Jordan came out another elevator flanked by two more sturdy-looking agents. Neal was wearing baggy jeans, a big fleece pullover, and a candy-striped stocking cap.

"Frank, man," he said in his totally relaxed way. "Early, huh?"

Frank grinned. "Can't wait to get on that ice wall."

DuBelle clicked her radio, and seconds later one of the black sport-utes and a two-car police escort rolled up in front of the hotel.

"That's handy," Frank said as he and Neal slid into the backseat. DuBelle joined Agent Ardis up front.

"It's one of the perks," Neal admitted.

Ardis steered them quickly through the quiet streets toward the stadium.

Neal slumped down in his seat, hands stuffed in his pockets, cap pulled down all the way to his eyebrows. Frank expected him to stay silent, but a few minutes into the ride, Neal started talking.

"Some of the stuff is cool," he said. "You know, about being the president's son and all that. It's like being on a cruise ship—all the food you can eat, whenever you want it. People dressing up and stuff all around you. There's an indoor pool, a gym. They even let me build a kickin' half-pipe on the East Lawn. That was sort of cool."

"What's not to like?" Frank asked.

Neal shrugged. "Being on a cruise ship all the time gets to be a drag. You know, the ship is nice, but you can't leave—you're in the middle of the stupid ocean."

"I think I get it," Frank said. "You like being the son of the president, but it stinks that you can never get away from it. You can never just go somewhere to be yourself."

Neal glanced at Frank. "Exactly, man. That's it exactly." He spoke in a low voice. "Last night wasn't the first time I got away from them."

Agent DuBelle looked over her shoulder and frowned at Neal.

"Once I climbed over the White House fence and went to see a late movie," Neal continued. "The only problem was, it was easier to break out than to break in. They caught me when I came home." He giggled. "You should've seen them, acting like I was some kind of terrorist trying to sneak into the White House. They were pretty embarrassed when they figured out it was me."

"You could have been shot," Agent DuBelle said angrily. "It wasn't funny."

Neal shrugged again and smiled. "I was laughing," he said.

Agent Ardis swung the truck into a parking lot across the street from the stadium. The ice-climbing wall had been set up over there, with its own temporary bleachers rising up on both sides of it.

Frank noticed the Hardys' van in the stadium lot. Joe was there, getting ready for the next round of snocross. Some spectators had already arrived and were waiting at the gate. Max Games employees hustled around getting things ready.

* * *

Back at the stadium, Joe threw his screwdriver across the pit area in frustration.

"Hey! Watch it there. You'll take someone's eye out!"

Joe looked up to see Amanda Mollica standing there, smiling.

"Morning, Amanda," he grumbled.

Amanda knelt down beside him. "What's the malfunction?"

"The right ski is all twisted up. I'll never get through the next round on this thing."

"You don't have a spare?"

Joe shook his head. "Edwards isn't the only one who doesn't have a sponsor," he said glumly. "I don't carry around a bunch of extra parts."

"Stay here," Amanda said, standing up. "I'll be right back."

She jogged off, and Joe went over to look for the screwdriver he'd thrown. He asked another competitor if he had a ski he could use. The guy said he was sorry, but no.

A few minutes later Amanda came jogging back around the corner, carrying a brand-new ski. She handed it to Joe.

Joe ran his hand over the smooth edge. "Wow. Thanks. Where'd you get it?"

Amanda didn't answer right away. "Hurry up," she said. "I heard them announce the first semifinal heat. You've got to get out there."

"Where did you get it?" Joe asked firmly.

Amanda stared at the floor. "I asked Jim Edwards for it," she admitted. "He said he felt bad about what happened last night and he wants you to have it."

Joe turned the part over in his hands. He didn't want to accept it, but the alternative was to drop out of the race. No way he was going to do that.

"Okay," he said finally. "Thanks. Tell Jim thanks."

Amanda smiled with relief. "I will," she said. "Good luck."

Twenty minutes later Joe pulled his snowmobile up to the starting line next to those of nine other drivers. He revved the engine, and it crackled with power.

As the green flag fell, Joe cranked the throttle and surged forward. He cut in, trying for the hole shot, but Edwards flashed by to take the lead going into the first turn.

Joe was in second gear as they roared up the big jump. He watched Edwards float up in front of him, then felt weightless for a second as he caught big air. He crashed to earth, using his legs to absorb the shock. Loose snow from Edwards's track shot back into his face, blocking his vision for a second.

The race continued like this—Edwards in front, cutting Joe off every time he tried to pass.

Coming around the last turn, Joe saw his chance. He crouched low on his sled and went to the outside.

Edwards swung out, bumping into Joe. Was Edwards trying to make him crash again? Joe gripped the handbars tight, but he could feel his snowmobile lose traction. He was out of control! He skidded violently right toward the stacked hay bales.

5 The End of the Rope

Joe leaned hard to the left. He was skimming along the hay bales at nearly thirty miles an hour. He hit a rise, and his snowmobile pitched savagely to the right. His repaired right ski had given out!

He slammed into the hay bales just in front of the finish line. The front of the sled caught between two bales as Joe felt himself go airborne.

He tried to hang on as the snowmobile turned two cartwheels, slamming end over end across the finish line.

The final jolt tore his grip from the handlebars, and Joe flew clear. He hit the track on his left shoulder and tumbled to a stop.

Instantly, he was up. He spun just in time to see

another competitor zooming straight for him. He dove for the hay bales.

The breeze of the speeding snowmobile washed over him as he safely cleared the bales. He hit the ground outside the snocross course and popped back to his feet.

Race officials were at his side in seconds. "You okay?" one asked.

Joe removed his helmet. "Fine," he growled. "Did I finish?"

An official laughed and slapped him on the back. "You came in second," he said. "But that's not the way I'd choose to cross the finish line."

Joe walked over to his snowmobile. It lay on its back like a giant dead bug. The replacement ski Edwards had given him was missing. Joe looked back down the course. There it was, lying in the snow right where Joe had lost control.

"He set me up!" Joe growled. He slammed his helmet into the ground and sprinted to the finish area.

Justice Edwards stood next to his snowmobile, signing autographs for a few fans. A camera crew stood by waiting to interview him.

Joe slowed to a stop a few yards from Jim. "Edwards!" he yelled. "You gave me a bad part!"

Edwards turned, a look of surprise on his face. "Get lost, Hardy. I whipped you fair and square."

Joe felt his face burn with rage. He lowered his

shoulder and barreled into Edwards, sending them both to the ground.

They rolled over a few times, each athlete struggling for an advantage.

Edwards tried to get Joe in a headlock. Joe tucked his chin close to his chest and smashed an uppercut into Jim's stomach.

Edwards groaned.

Joe stood up, grabbing Edwards by the collar of his riding suit. He lifted him up and slammed him into the ground again.

He was about to do it again, when four or five pairs of hands pulled him away.

"Chill out!" another racer shouted. "Fight's over, man."

Two snocross competitors helped Edwards to his feet. Joe twisted free of the guys holding him and pointed his finger at Jim. "That's twice you've tried to knock me out of the race!" he shouted. "It won't happen again."

"You're a loser!" Edwards shot back. "Deal with it."

Race officials jumped between the two. "Shut up!" one of them said. "I'll disqualify both of you if you keep this up."

Fred Vale came jogging over. "I'll take care of this," he told the other officials. "Go on, get the next heat set up."

When everyone had cleared out, Vale congratulated Edwards on a good race, then put an arm around Joe's shoulders and led him away from the finish area.

"You and Edwards are doing great. You're the stars of the Max Games so far, man," he said. Then he lowered his voice to a whisper. "Whatever you need for your snowmobile, I'll get it for you before the finals."

Joe froze. It didn't seem fair that the contest organizer would help one athlete. "No thanks," he said. "I'll get it fixed myself."

"Whatever," Vale said, standing back. "I don't care how you do it, just keep this rivalry stoked." He pointed at Joe. "Let me know if you need anything, Joe. It's yours."

Joe watched Vale go over to the camera crew to get some more face time on the local news. Then Joe went back to get his helmet and see about his damaged snowmobile.

Earlier Frank and Neal had arrived at the ice-climbing venue. Frank carried his backpack, while Neal hauled a nylon duffel containing his snowboard and boots.

Metal barriers were set up in a forty-foot square with the ice wall at one end. Two or three large portable bleachers were set up outside each side of the square.

Only athletes were allowed inside the barriers; after Neal and Frank showed their IDs they went in and sat on a bench.

47

Neal gazed up at the fifty-foot wall. The face rose straight up, but the ice was rough and full of cracks, tiny ledges, and bumps, just like those on a real mountain.

"Freaky" was all Neal said.

"It takes them a week to get it set up," Frank said, pulling ice axes out of his pack. "Basically, it's a big set of scaffolding with cooling pipes running through it. They pump water through tubes to the top, and the water runs down the face of the wall slowly and freezes."

Frank noticed that Agents Ardis and DuBelle were remaining in the background. Frank couldn't hear them, but he could see them constantly talking on their radios, directing other agents to move from one place to another.

Frank continued. "To change the shape of the wall they have different pieces they can attach to it. When the water freezes over them it makes a step or a crack."

"But what if one side is easier to climb than the other?"

"Each race is two heats," Frank said. "You go up one side while your opponent goes up the other. Then you switch sides. Lowest total time wins."

As Neal nodded his understanding, two more climbers arrived.

Jamal threw his bag down next to the bench. "What's up, Frank?" He gestured to the guy who'd come in with him. " 'The Claw' here says he's going to show us how it's done."

Frank instantly recognized Rick "The Claw" Salazar, the top climber on the circuit. He was about Joe's height, six feet, but lanky and incredibly flexible. He wore his shoulder-length black hair pulled back in a ponytail, and a tiny gold ice-ax earring hung from his left ear.

Frank introduced Neal to Jamal and Rick.

"I thought I recognized you," Rick said. "Sammy said you were competing in the aerials."

"Yup."

Salazar held up his fist and glanced at Jamal. "President's kid shreds. That's sick, man—I can't wait to see it."

Jamal nodded. "That's going to be a wild contest."

Frank could tell Neal was enjoying the attention. He pulled his steel crampons from his bag and carefully clipped them to his boots. "Who's going to test this wall?" he asked.

"I made a few runs last night," Jamal said, sitting on the bench next to Neal. "It's sort of sketchy toward the top. Slick as glass."

"Good," Salazar said. "You got first, Jamal. Show us the route."

When Jamal had his gear on, the four athletes walked over to the wall. A safety harness hung down from the top by two nylon ropes. A pulley system would catch Jamal if he slipped off the wall.

Jamal stepped into the harness and ran the rope through his belt. He gave it a sharp tug to make certain it was anchored, then asked Frank to hand him his ice axes.

"Now show us your scoot," Salazar said.

Jamal looped one ax over a hook on his belt, then swung the other at the wall. The pick end stuck tight in a narrow fissure.

Using his free hand to balance against the wall, Jamal pulled himself up. He jammed the sharp tips of his crampons into the ice.

With a few deft moves, he was twenty feet off the ground. Then he seemed to get stuck.

"There's a fissure above your left hand," Frank called.

Hanging on the wall like an insect, Jamal reached up as high as he could and jammed the flat adze end of his ax into the fissure. He pulled himself sideways and up, then suddenly fumbled for a foothold. He slipped down a couple of feet, snapping the rope tight.

"Ha!" Salazar shouted. "On a free climb you'd splat, Hawkins."

"If I fall, I'm gonna make sure it's right on your head, Rick," Jamal answered.

Jamal wasn't stalled for long. Once he maneuvered around a big bulge in the ice, it was easy climbing to the top.

He stood up on the edge and tossed the safety harness down. "Who's next?"

Salazar grabbed the harness. "Get out your stop-watch, Hardy," he said. "You're about to see a new record."

Within seconds Salazar was halfway up the wall. So many ice chips were flying that Frank and Neal had to step back and shield their eyes as they watched him.

Jamal appeared, having climbed down the ladder at the back of the wall. "How's he doing?"

"He's moving," Neal said. "It's like he's memorized the whole thing."

Salazar took the wall in big chunks, reaching far over his head with one arm to sink his ax, then pulling up and hammering the other one in above it.

He pulled himself over the top ledge and looked down, smirking. "Here you go, Frank," he said. "Let's see what you've got."

The harness landed at Frank's feet.

"Take your time, Frank," Jamal said. "Don't let him psych you out."

Frank clipped on the harness and dug his axes into the wall. He hoisted himself up, scooted side-ways a foot or so, then started to climb along a small crevasse he had discovered.

"The ice is good," he said to Jamal. "Not too soft, not too brittle."

"Yeah," Jamal said. "Wait till you get to the top. It's not so nice there."

"How's it going, Frank?" Salazar yelled from

above. "I'm timing you with a sundial up here, man."

Frank ignored Rick. He looked away from the wall for a moment. He was now about thirty feet up, he guessed. A few spectators were sitting in the bleachers, watching the athletes practice.

Frank came to a big bulge in the ice. He couldn't see the top now; it was like being under a ledge. The safest thing to do would be to go around it, as Jamal had done. But it might be faster to go right over it.

Reaching back over his head, Frank smashed his ax into the bulge. Splinters of ice rained down on him. He tugged. The ax seemed secure.

Frank made sure his feet were set, then slammed the other ax into the ice. Now came the tricky part. He would have to let go with his feet. Then he would be hanging in midair by the ax handles. To get over the ledge he would have to use only his arms, pulling each ax out in turn and hammering it back into the wall—like climbing a Peg-Board.

He let his feet fall free.

"Keep going, Frank," Jamal shouted. "You got it, buddy."

Salazar's teasing voice floated down. "You stuck, Frank? Need a ladder?"

Frank pulled the left ax free. Now he hung by one hand. With all his strength, he pulled up and punched the left ax back in as high as he could. It was going well. He'd be over in a few more seconds.

He felt a tug on the rope. Probably nothing, he thought.

Frank reached the top of the ledge. Getting both axes set tight, he concentrated on lifting his right leg up over the edge. Then he would be all the way over.

When he thought he had his crampons dug in well, he tried to pull himself up. He put pressure on his foot.

The ice gave way. His foot lost its grip and swung free. He felt the axes break loose.

Now he was falling. Frank waited for the safety line to stop him. It went tight, snapping his head. Then, just as suddenly, it slackened.

He was falling again. Falling thirty feet to the cold pavement below.

6 Daring Aerials

Frank could see the rope slithering through the pulley on his harness like a snake. If it all pulled through, he'd be dead. Acting on instinct, Frank dropped the ice ax from his right hand and grabbed the cord.

He stopped abruptly and slammed into the wall. Spinning slowly, Frank looked down. He guessed he was still twenty, maybe twenty-five feet up.

"Frank!" Jamal shouted. "What happened?"

"The rope came loose up on top," Frank said, trying to catch his breath and slow his pounding heart. He checked the harness. The friction of the rope had almost burned through his climbing glove. His hand ached from the effort of holding on.

"I can't hold on much longer," he said. "If I lose my grip, I'm going to fall."

As he spun, Frank caught glimpses of Jamal's and Neal's frightened faces. And there was Agent DuBelle, speaking rapidly into her radio.

He felt the rope slipping slowly through his fingers. Kicking out desperately, he managed to get one crampon jammed into the ice wall. That stopped the spinning, at least.

With his left hand, he hacked at the wall with his remaining ice ax. Nothing. It wouldn't stick. He tried again. It grabbed and held.

At that instant, the rope slipped away. Frank found himself on the wall with no safety rope and only one ice ax.

"Hardy! You still on the wall?" It was Salazar calling down from the top.

"He's stuck," Jamal shouted. "What happened up there?"

"No clue," Salazar said. "Frank, you going back down?"

Frank had two fingers of his free hand wedged into a tiny crack. He took a deep breath. "I'm coming up," he said. He noticed a crowd gathering below him.

"Your call, Frank," Salazar replied.

This time Frank went around the ledge. He set the pick of the ax in his left hand tight in the ice. Then he used the fingers on his handlike pitons, jamming them into any fissure he could find, and pulled himself up.

His arms shook with the effort, and sweat poured down his face. He climbed slowly, searching blindly with his feet for any foothold.

"A few more feet," Salazar called. "I'm sending down a new rope."

Frank found a nice seam and followed it up. When he saw Salazar's rope in front of him, he ignored it. He'd rather complete the climb without help, he decided.

He reached the top, and Salazar grabbed him under one arm and pulled him to his feet.

The crowd below clapped.

"Gutsy climb," Jamal shouted up at him.

"What happened up here?" Frank asked.

Rick patted him on the back. "Dude, it was bad luck. Those ropes just gave out. They were fine when I went up."

"Yeah. Bad luck is right," Frank said.

Salazar smiled. "You need a parachute for this sport, man. A lot safer that way."

"Let me have a look at that rope."

Salazar quickly pulled the rope up, coiling it neatly. He pretended to hand it to Frank, then tossed it over the edge.

"Oops. Sorry, Frank."

Frank started to say something, but Salazar immediately pulled out his ice axes and started back down the wall without the safety harness.

"You coming, Frank?" he asked, grinning mischievously. "I'll race you down."

Frank watched him disappear over the edge. "No thanks, Rick. I'll take the ladder." He walked across the top platform to the back of the wall, where a ladder was set up.

Neal, Jamal, and Agent DuBelle met Frank back on the ground.

"What went on up there?" Jamal asked.

"No idea," Frank replied. "I'd like to take a look at that rope, though." He hurried around to the front of the wall.

Fred Vale had arrived and had the coil of rope in his hands. He and another Max Games official rushed up to Frank.

"I heard what happened," Vale said. "You're not hurt, are you?"

"I'm okay," Frank replied, holding his hand out for the rope.

Vale pulled it away. "Nope. Sorry, friend. Nobody touches this but me."

"That piece of equipment almost got me killed," Frank said angrily. "Let me see it."

Vale looked over Frank's shoulder at Jamal, Neal, and DuBelle. It seemed as though he wanted to yell back at Frank but was restraining himself.

"Look," he said, keeping his voice low. "I promise I'll personally test every piece of Max Games equipment. But nobody can hear about this, okay. I *do not* skimp on safety equipment."

Frank turned away in disgust. "Come on," he said to Neal and Jamal. "Let's get out of here."

As they packed up their stuff, Frank looked around for Salazar. He wasn't around, and no one seemed to have seen him since he'd climbed down the wall.

Neal said he was hungry, so they headed back over to the snack area at the stadium. They walked past a crowd outside the stadium parking lot, waiting to catch shuttle buses.

"What's up with this crowd?" Neal asked.

"Some events, like say, downhill mountain biking and maximum biathlon, are held at sites outside town," Jamal answered. "A shuttle bus is the best way to get there."

"Maximum biathlon?"

"Yeah," Frank said. "You ride a snowmobile through the woods really fast and stop every mile or so to shoot targets with an air rifle."

Neal turned to Agent DuBelle, who was hanging back, as usual. "Sounds like an event for you," he teased.

Agent DuBelle sent back a fake smile. "Sure, Neal. I'll sign right up."

They all laughed.

As Frank might have guessed, they found Joe in the snack area munching on a chili dog.

When Frank, Jamal, and Neal finally sat down with their food, Joe told them about his run-in with Jim Edwards.

"Fred Vale was totally amped about it," he said. "He was happy we got into a fight."

Frank nodded and related his own adventure on the ice wall. "Vale showed up there, too," he said. "At first he seemed concerned, but when I asked to look at the rope he got all mad about it and told me to keep quiet."

"I don't know," Jamal said, taking a gulp of soda. "You really think Vale's so desperate for ratings that he'd endanger the lives of the athletes?"

"All I know is that he was happy I wiped out," Joe said.

Frank grabbed a bunch of fries. "Either the safety rope was bad or Rick Salazar tried to snuff me."

Neal's eyes grew wide. "Attempted murder?"

"Come on, Frank," Jamal said. "Salazar's competitive, but you don't think he'd go that far, do you?"

"He was the only one on top of the wall," Frank said.

Joe shrugged. "Jim Edwards sends me into the hay bales twice. Frank almost falls from the ice wall. Something's going on, and I think we need to do some serious investigating."

"If I could get a look at that rope, it might tell us something," Frank said.

"And Vale's finances," Joe said. "We should see how deep in the hole he really is."

The teens finished eating in silence. When they

were done, Neal asked if they would go watch him practice some jumps.

"Sounds great," Joe said.

They started to get up, but Agent DuBelle made them wait about fifteen minutes while she had other agents check out the snowboard area.

"See?" Neal said. "It's a big drag."

At last they were allowed to walk over to the soccer field next to the stadium.

The jump tower rose from the middle of the snowy field. Built of wood and steel rails, the tower rose nearly forty feet from the ground. The ramp swooped down from the top like a big letter *J*. A huge mound of snow sloped away from the lip of the ramp, providing a perfect landing zone.

A little hut at the top of the tower allowed jumpers who were waiting for their turns to hang out and stay warm.

While Neal put on his boots, they watched other snowboarders practice their jumps.

A jumper in a tasseled cap appeared at the door of the jump hut.

"You guys gotta watch this dude," Neal said. "That's Twist Winiki. He's the boss."

The rider got himself square, then let go of the handrails. He turned from side to side to control his speed, then straightened out as he approached the end of the ramp.

He held his arms out at his sides, then tucked

them close to his body as he took off. He rose high into the air, spinning like a majorette's baton.

He completed three backflips with three full twists, then landed perfectly.

Neal whistled and cheered.

"Can you beat that?" Joe asked.

"I'll try," Neal said, marching off with his board under his arm.

A minute or two later it was Neal's turn. He pushed himself out of the hut and centered his board on the ramp.

"Quad-quad!" Frank shouted, calling for the almost impossible quadruple flip with a quadruple twist.

Neal dismissed him with a laugh and a wave of his hand. Letting go of the railings, he tore down the ramp.

Neal zoomed off the ramp into a front flip. When he completed the flip, he was still going higher into the air. At the highest point, he went into a half-twist, then did two back flips and another half-twist on the way down.

He nailed the landing and raised his arms over his head.

"Radical!" Joe shouted.

"Wow!" Jamal agreed. "He's got talent."

Neal hurried over and glided to a stop, his face flushed with excitement. "Like it?"

Frank held out his forearm, and Neal bashed his

into it. "A front half, double back half," Frank said. "That's a medal jump for sure."

"Thanks, man."

Neal was about to climb the ladder for another jump when a murmur went through the crowd of spectators.

Neal's eyebrows shot up. "Something going on?"

"I don't know," Frank said.

They watched as people started running across the field and over to the stadium parking lot.

"What's up?" Joe asked, grabbing at someone's arm. The person didn't answer.

The teens, surrounded by the Secret Service agents, went with the crowd.

When they got to the parking lot, Frank looked up. Instantly he stopped in his tracks.

Joe almost bumped into him. "What in the world—" He followed Frank's gaze up to the rim of the stadium.

There, on the narrow railing around the upper deck, stood three figures.

"No way!" Joe said. It was hard to make them out from that distance, but the three people were definitely Sammy Fear, Amanda Mollica, and Rick Salazar. "How high up are they?"

"A hundred and fifty feet, easy," Frank said.

A Max Games security guard held a megaphone to his lips. "Don't jump!" he said. "Step back from the railing before someone gets hurt!"

"Stay clear!" Sammy Fear yelled, his voice

sounding tinny and small from so high up. "I'm going to jump and no one can stop me!"

Frank watched as Fred Vale and a cameraman muscled their way through the crowd to get a better view.

Rick Salazar tossed something into the air. The crowd reacted, then calmed down as everyone realized that it was a rope.

"Are they going to climb down?" Jamal asked.

Before anyone answered, Salazar hooked on to the rope and rappelled down the outside wall of the stadium like an Airborne Ranger dropping from a helicopter.

He hit the ground and stepped back a few steps from the wall. "Come on down!" he shouted to Fear and Mollica.

Without hooking on to the rope, they launched themselves into space.

7 The Imposter

People in the crowd screamed.

Frank didn't want to look, but he couldn't pull his eyes away. As Fear and Mollica jumped, he saw each of them throw something clear.

They plummeted in the classic skydiving position—arms out, legs spread-eagled.

Frank squinted against the glare of the sun. The objects they'd thrown trailed above them as they fell, then popped open.

"BASE-jumping chutes!" Frank shouted. He watched the canopies open completely. Fear and Mollica were using the compact, quick-opening chutes that enthusiasts used when they jumped from stationary objects like buildings and bridges.

Neal's jaw dropped open as Fear and Mollica once again drifted safely down over the crowd.

People in the crowd followed them as if mesmerized. When the two jumpers landed at the far end of the parking lot, they were quickly overwhelmed by fans and security guards.

"Wow! That was totally amazing," Neal said. He pushed his way through the crowd, obviously determined to talk to Sammy Fear.

Joe watched as Agent DuBelle grabbed Neal's arm and asked him to stop.

Then, from out of nowhere, Agent Ardis stepped in and cleared a path for the president's son. "Let him have some fun," Ardis said.

Frank, sensing his opportunity, dropped back and headed for the stadium wall. He found the rope hanging where Salazar had rappelled down.

He couldn't see anything wrong with it. The rope looked similar to the one at the ice wall, but there was no way to be sure.

Joe and Jamal followed Neal and the Secret Service agents through the crowd. By the time they got to Fear and Mollica, Fred Vale was already there. Security guys were holding fans back, while Vale interviewed Fear on camera.

Looking over, the promoter spotted Neal. He smiled broadly into the camera. "Look," he said, "it's the most famous participant in the Max Games. Come over here, Neal."

Vale pulled Neal over next to Fear and Mollica. "What'd you think of that stunt?"

Fear and Neal exchanged high fives. "That was wild!" Neal shouted. "How'd it feel, man?"

"Trippy, man," Fear said. "All these faces were looking up at us all worried. What a total hoot!"

Vale shoved the microphone at Mollica. She blushed. "I guess it was fun," she said, hesitating. "I was pretty nervous."

Vale lost interest in her and went back to Neal and Fear, who were now acting like best friends.

Fear put an arm around Neal's shoulder. Escorted by Max Games security and Secret Service agents, they made their way through the crowd to the athletes' lounge under the stadium. Frank joined them there.

Once the security guards had cleared out, Fear turned to Agent DuBelle.

"Neal asked me if I'd hang with him at his snowboard competition this afternoon," he said. "Is that cool?"

Neal looked at DuBelle hopefully.

The agent crossed her arms. "I don't know, Neal. Things are getting out of hand around here."

Agent Ardis spoke up. "I think it's okay," he said. "We've got plenty of agents on duty, and Frank and Joe will be there."

Joe leaned in, "I've got to work on my sled. Sorry, Neal. Wish I could be there."

"It's okay," Neal said. It was clear he was willing

to trade Joe for Sammy Fear. He looked at DuBelle. "Let Sammy be there instead of Joe."

Michelle frowned. "Okay, but no antics."

Both Sammy and Neal nodded vigorously.

Joe stuck his hand out to shake with Neal. "Good luck. I'll catch up with you later."

But Neal and Fear were already yammering about the BASE jump and the aerial contest.

As Joe started out of the room, Frank pulled him over. "You need help getting your sled together, bro?"

"I should be okay. Stick around here and keep an eye on our daredevil friend there," he said, nodding toward Fear. "I don't trust him."

"I'll help you wrench your sled," Jamal said.

"Thanks."

Joe and Jamal headed back to the snocross pit area.

A couple of hours later, at around two in the afternoon, Frank, Sammy, Neal, and a group of agents arrived at the snowboard jump.

The stands were packed now, and everyone cheered as Fear and Neal walked past the bleachers. Fear waved up at the crowd, then blew kisses at the contest judges, who sat in a special box in the front row.

The three teens sat down on a heated bench next to the jump tower. Other snowboarders paced nervously or sat, quietly concentrating on the jumps they would soon perform. Twist Winiki sat far from everyone else, studying the edge of his board.

Contest officials walked around, speaking quietly to each athlete. A young woman carrying a clipboard came up to their bench. "Neal Jordan?" she asked, looking at Neal's number bib.

"Yeah," Neal answered.

"You'll be jumping fourth," she said. "You can go up to the hut when there are two jumpers ahead of you."

"Can I go up with him?" Fear asked.

"Are you his coach?"

Neal and Fear glanced at each other. "Yes," Neal answered. "He's my coach."

"Sure. Then you can go up."

Neal nodded and the official moved on to the next athlete.

"Okay," Fear said to Neal. "Remember what I told you, man. Visualize yourself nailing the jump."

"Right." Neal stood up and did some stretches.

A few minutes later the announcer called the names of the first three jumpers and told them to climb the tower and report in at the jump hut.

Neal didn't want to watch the jumpers in front of him, but Frank was excited to see the competition.

"Number one, jump when ready," the announcer bellowed. The crowd went silent.

Frank looked up to see a figure in loose-fitting ski pants and a sweatshirt step out of the hut door. The guy adjusted his goggles, then headed down the ramp.

He pulled off a double layout back flip but touched his hand on the landing.

"Decent jump," Fear said. "Little sketchy on the landing, but decent."

"You can go up to the hut now," Frank said to Neal. "You're third in line."

Neal pulled his helmet and goggles from his duffel bag. He pinned his number bib to his fleece pullover and headed up the ladder. Fear followed.

The next jumper was unspectacular. He performed a basic flip, double twist, and botched the landing, falling on his butt and sliding all the way down the landing slope.

Low scores flashed on an electronic board.

Frank spotted Agent DuBelle standing behind the crowd barrier. She looked up into the hut intently.

The jumper just before Neal was Twist Winiki, from Hawaii. Now we'll see some serious jumping, Frank said to himself.

Winiki stepped from the hut and raised his arms over his head. He seemed to be going over the jump in his mind.

Then he zipped down the ramp in a blur of speed. He hit the lip of the ramp and shot into the air, spinning so fast Frank couldn't count the rotations.

Somehow, Winiki made himself stop flipping and

spinning at the perfect time. He opened up out of his tuck and executed a smooth, brilliant landing.

The crowd jumped up for a standing ovation.

The scores were nearly perfect.

"Okay, Neal," Frank mumbled. "Concentrate. Nail this thing."

Neal appeared at the top of the ramp, looking much thinner and younger than the more experienced Winiki. He stood quietly for a moment, then started down.

He did the same jump he'd practiced, a front half, double back half.

Frank clenched his fists as he watched Neal turn through the air. "Get the landing, Neal!" he shouted.

Neal opened up a fraction of a second too early. He didn't rotate far enough and landed on the nose of his board.

For a split second he held on. Frank sucked in a breath.

Then Neal went down, skidding down the slope on his face.

Frank groaned.

Sammy Fear climbed down from the tower and met Neal when he came back around.

Neal looked as though he was about to cry.

"Suck it up," Fear said. "You barely missed it, man."

"Tough luck," Frank added. "I thought you had it nailed."

Neal couldn't answer. He flopped down on the bench and waited for the scores.

Frank watched the numbers flash on. "Well," he said, "they liked the jump, but the landing cost you. You'll just have to stick the next one."

Neal looked down at his boots.

They watched as the rest of the athletes jumped. By the time the first round was over, Neal was stuck in eleventh place.

"I might as well drop out," Neal grumbled. "I don't have any chance for a medal now."

"Don't quit," Fear said. "Stick it out. That's the way you get stronger."

Frank handed Neal his helmet. "Get back up there."

The announcer started the second round, and Neal and Fear trudged back up the ladder to the hut.

Again, the first two jumpers weren't very good. The announcer even had to scold the crowd when people stopped paying attention and started talking amongst themselves.

When it was Winiki's turn, everyone paid attention.

This time he concentrated even longer than usual. One of the other jumpers mouthed the words "quad-quad" to Frank.

Frank signaled thumbs up. That jump was something he'd like to see.

Winiki pushed off the railing, sending himself

71

down faster than any other jumper. He rocketed into the air, twisting and flipping even as his board left the ramp.

The twists went too fast, but Frank could count the flips. "One, two, three, four—"

Winiki slammed into the landing ramp. He hit so hard that his knees buckled and he almost sat all the way down.

Frank grimaced, then relaxed as Winiki got the landing under control and schussed down the slope.

The crowd went nuts again. They cheered until the scores came up. Then they cheered even louder. A perfect score!

Frank hoped the jump would inspire Neal. Maybe he could work his way into the top ten. That would be great for someone his age, Frank thought.

After a long wait, he saw Neal come out of the hut. He pulled his helmet strap tight.

Frank stood up to get a better view. Neal looked taller and thinner all the way up there.

Neal steered his way down the ramp. This time he performed a beautiful triple twisting gainer. He opened out of his tuck and landed lightly, gracefully, like a bird settling on a lawn.

The crowd roared.

Frank glanced over at Agent DuBelle. Her brow wrinkled. She stared at Neal, a look of confusion on her face.

Frank realized what was wrong. That jumper

wasn't Neal! He had on Neal's helmet and pullover. But that person was too tall to be Neal.

"You!" Agent DuBelle shouted. "Take off that helmet now!"

The imposter released his bindings, stepped off his board, and took off running.

8 The Invitation

The snowboarder wearing Neal's number raced away from Frank, passing right in front of Agent DuBelle. She grabbed for his pullover but missed.

"Stop! Halt!" she yelled. Placing one hand on the top rail, she vaulted the barrier and gave chase.

Frank looked up. Another snowboarder, unaware of all the commotion, had stepped out of the hut to jump. It wasn't Neal, so Frank ran for the ladder at the back of the tower.

Ken Ardis jumped a barrier and fell in behind Frank. They stopped at the base of the ladder.

"Is he up there?" Ardis asked.

Frank was about to start climbing when he noticed a slender figure walking casually around the other side of the tower. He recognized Sammy's leather sponsor's jacket.

Frank fell into a sprint and shouted for the officials at the athletes' entrance to stop the guy.

He saw the figure slip through the gate. "Stop him!" he yelled. If the person made it into the crowd, they'd never find him.

An official stepped in front of the guy. Frank came up, put his hand on the person's shoulder, and spun him around.

It was Neal.

Ardis grabbed Neal under the arm roughly. "What is going on, young man?"

Neal seemed bewildered, a little confused. "I—I was going for a walk, I guess."

"A walk!" Ardis marched Neal back to the bench behind the jump tower.

Frank could feel the entire crowd watching them. He saw Neal's face go red with embarrassment.

When they got back to the athletes' area, Agent DuBelle was already there with the imposter. It was Sammy Fear. She shoved him down on the bench.

An official came up and quietly asked if everything was all right.

"Fine," DuBelle said. "We apologize. Go ahead and restart the competition."

The official nodded and hustled away.

DuBelle turned to Neal. "What kind of stunt was that?"

Neal scratched his head. "I don't know. I guess I was bummed about my jump. I just felt like taking off."

"No, no," Fear said, waving his hand in the air. "It was all my idea, man. I figured it'd be a hoot. I do a jump, Neal takes a walk, everybody gets a big laugh. He wasn't going to go far, were you, Neal?"

"Um. No, I don't think so."

Frank waited for Ardis to explode, but the agent's attitude suddenly changed. He took a step back and smiled. Then he let out a hearty laugh.

"Either you're very brave or very stupid," he said to Fear, shaking his head. "That was a good way to get yourself shot."

"Or at least arrested," DuBelle snapped. "In fact, I've got a mind to haul you in right now."

Agent Ardis rebuttoned his overcoat. "They were just having fun. I don't think we should make too much out of it."

"Since when did you go soft?" DuBelle asked.

Ardis smiled. "I don't want Neal to think I'm a hard case all the time."

Neal stood there, watching the exchange in silence. He took off Sammy's jacket and handed it back to him. "Can I have my pullover, man?"

"Sure thing," Fear said. "Hey, little prez. You want to help me and Amanda go over our sky-surfing gig?"

76

"Uh, I don't know," Neal said, turning to Frank. "What are you gonna do now, Frank?"

"I was going to go help my brother get his sled together." Frank checked his watch. "The snocross finals are in less than an hour."

"Can I go with you?"

Everyone, especially Frank, was surprised that Neal didn't want to hang out with Sammy anymore.

"Sure," Frank said. "I'm sure he could use the extra help."

Neal said goodbye to Sammy and packed up his snowboard and other gear. Then Ardis and another stocky agent led the way back to the stadium, while DuBelle hung behind.

As they approached the tunnel leading under the stadium, Frank looked back over his shoulder.

When he was satisfied that DuBelle was out of earshot, he said, "So, Neal, I figured you'd be dying to help Sammy with his routine. What's up?"

Neal stuffed his hands in his pockets. "I don't know, man. I didn't feel like it, that's all."

"Whose idea was it, really, to pull that stunt?"

"It was Sammy's idea," Neal said. "I guess that weirded me out a little."

"How come?" They passed into the tunnel and headed toward the snocross pit area.

"Because I wasn't just going for a walk, like Sammy said. It was a whole big plan. I was supposed to sneak away and go find Amanda all the way on the other side of the stadium."

"What for?"

"He said she was going to let me in on a big stunt they'd planned."

"What kind of stunt?"

Neal switched his duffel from one hand to the other. "I asked, but he wouldn't say."

The whole situation seemed kind of strange to Frank, but before he had time to ask Neal more questions, they ran into Joe and Fred Vale. A cameraman was right behind them.

Vale held the microphone under Joe's nose. "Do you have your snowmobile all tweaked out for the finals, Joe?"

Joe stared hard into the camera. "I've got a few more things I can do to get extra horsepower," he said. "But I'll be ready by race time."

"How about Justice Edwards? You nervous about going up against him again in the finals after those two big wipeouts?"

Frank saw his brother's jaw muscles twitch at the mention of Edwards's name.

"No way," Joe said. "I'm ready for anything he's got. Tell him to bring it on."

"Great!" Vale said, motioning for the cameraman to stop filming. "Great interview, Joe. Good luck in the finals."

Vale and the cameraman hurried off in the direction of Edwards's pit.

"Hey, fellas," Joe said. "Neal, man. How'd the jumping go?"

When Neal didn't say anything, Frank spoke for him. "Pretty good. He almost had a top-ten finish, but he doesn't want to talk about it. Where's Jamal?"

"He had to go help his dad get the planes ready for the sky surfing tomorrow," Joe said, stepping back over to his snowmobile. "Vale wasted a lot of my time. I've got to rush to get ready."

The three of them made some final adjustments to the sled. Then it was time to help Joe push it out to the course.

Frank and Neal sat in the same seats they'd had the night before. Frank tried to pick out the Secret Service agents around them, but this time they weren't so obvious.

Down on the track, Joe idled his sled up to the starting line. This was what he lived for. The stands were full of fans. It was late afternoon and getting dark, and the stadium lights would click on at any minute. He loved racing under the lights; it made him feel as if he was going extra fast.

He looked to his right, down the line of racers. Edwards was three places away from him, but Joe expected him to come flying across his path at the start. That maniac would do anything to get a hole shot.

Joe cranked the throttle. His sled sounded good. The ski was fixed. The race was his.

The green flag fell, and Joe bolted for the first turn.

Everything became a blur. He could feel someone coming up on his right, but he didn't dare look over. One second of lapsed concentration could send him skidding out of control.

He felt something knock against him as he leaned into the first turn. He was in front! He had the lead!

Then a sled slammed into him from the right. Pain shot up his leg. He looked over. It was Edwards. The light green sled came at him again, trying to run him off the track.

Joe's souped-up machine was faster going up the jumps. He pulled ahead slightly.

It was a two-man race. Edwards took the lead for a lap, then Joe stole it away again. They were dead even heading to the last jump. Joe crouched down to cut wind resistance and opened the throttle wide. He blasted into the air. Whoever jumped farther would take the race.

Joe was so high up he had to look down to his left to see the race official waving the checkered flag. He hit the ground less than a foot in front of Edwards. He'd won!

The crowd stood up and cheered. Joe took a victory lap, standing up on his snowmobile and holding one fist in the air.

By the time he pulled off the track, Vale was already interviewing Jim Edwards.

Joe pulled his helmet off and went over to shake Jim's hand. Vale stepped between them, holding the microphone as usual.

"Joe Hardy. Edwards says his snowmobile wasn't running well. What do you think? Did you get lucky and catch him on an off night?"

"I don't know anything about that," Joe said. He tried to push past Vale. "Jim. Good race, man."

"Forget you!" Edwards shouted. "That race was mine!"

Vale stepped away, perhaps hoping for a fight.

Joe waved his hands at Edwards dismissively. "Whatever, man. Good race anyway."

Vale grunted and dropped the microphone to his side. He looked at his cameraman. "Maybe we'll get some better fireworks between these two at the medal ceremony tonight," he said.

Joe went back to his sled. Frank and Neal were there. "Awesome race," Neal shouted. "You smoked him!"

"Yeah," Frank said. "It looked like he tried to knock you off the course again, but this time you were too strong."

"Thanks, guys," Joe said. "I have to admit that revenge does feel good."

They pushed Joe's snowmobile back under the stands. When DuBelle and Ardis showed up to take Neal back to his hotel, Neal reminded Frank about his family's being on vacation in the Catskills.

"Yeah, I remember," Frank said. "You said you were going to join them after the Max Games."

"There's been a change in plans," DuBelle said. "We're going tonight."

Agent Ardis frowned. "I don't see why they should know this."

Neal ignored him. "It would be excellent if you guys could come visit after the games," Neal said. "You could tell me all about the sky surfing, since I'm going to miss it."

Both Frank and Joe were about to answer an enthusiastic yes, when Ardis tried to nix the idea.

"Absolutely not," he said. "We'd have to clear it with the president and the chief of security first."

"I'm the chief of security," DuBelle said. "And I clear the visit."

"All right!" Neal shouted. "Cool. I'll see you guys later then."

The Hardys said goodbye and watched Neal lope off, surrounded by Secret Service agents.

Twenty minutes later Joe had all his stuff packed up and ready to go.

"I'll pull the van around behind the stadium," Frank said. "Then we can hook up the trailer and load your snowmobile."

"I'll meet you out there," Joe replied.

Frank jogged to the parking lot. It was about six in the evening—dark now, though the moon was almost full. He jumped in the van and drove around behind the stadium. A row of snowmobile trailers were parked along the outer wall. No one else seemed to be loading up yet.

Frank backed the van up to their trailer, then

hopped out. Joe was waiting at the double doors. He slowly piloted the sled out the doors and up onto the ramp.

Using chains and padlocks, he swiftly secured the sled to the trailer.

"Ready," he said.

Frank got in the driver's seat. "Let's get home and eat."

"I second that motion," Joe answered, clambering in the passenger side.

Frank was about to turn the key when a tremendous bang echoed through the van. The roof over Joe's head buckled and creased.

Frank's eyes went wide. "What? Someone's up there, Joe!"

They heard the sound of metal ripping, and the gleaming blade of an ice ax punctured the roof.

Joe grabbed for the ax head, but it disappeared.

The night went silent.

"Where'd he go?" Joe whispered.

The answer came quickly. An ax-shaped shadow passed over the windshield, then Frank's side window exploded in on him.

9 Soft Target

Frank threw up his arm to shield his eyes from the flying glass.

"We're sitting ducks!" Joe shouted. "Get out of the van." He opened his door and rolled to the ground. He scrambled to his feet in front of the van.

A man wearing a snocross helmet with a shaded visor dropped lightly from the roof. He faced Joe, holding the ice ax in the air like a club.

Frank jumped from the van and ran to his brother's side. "It's two against one," he said. "I'll take those odds."

The Hardys heard a muffled laugh. "Try two against two," a voice said.

Frank watched as a second thug appeared from

the darkness. He swung the heavy rubber track of a snowmobile over his head. The tiny steel spikes that helped the tread grip the snow sparkled in the moonlight.

"Uh-oh," Joe said. "We're in trouble."

The thug with the ice ax leaped forward and took a chopping swing at Joe.

Joe ducked and heard the blade whistle beside his ear. He nailed the guy with a short punch to the ribs, then danced away.

The other thug faked swinging the track at Frank, then smashed a front kick into his chest.

Frank staggered back. He couldn't get air. All he knew was that he had to keep his balance. His attacker stepped forward. Frank saw the track moving toward him. He lifted his left arm to block it.

The blow felt like being hit with a chair. Frank fell to the ground, his cheek and jaw thumping with pain.

He looked up. The thug was standing over him, track held high.

"You won't be baby-sitting Neal Jordan anymore," the man growled.

Then it seemed as if a spotlight lit up his attacker. The guy quickly darted out of the light.

Frank heard footsteps as the two men ran away. "Joe?"

"Are you okay, Frank? Can you stand?"

Frank felt himself nod. He was still groggy, but he stood up.

He found himself facing the headlights of a pickup truck. Those must have been the spotlights, he said to himself.

A young man Frank recognized as a snocross competitor stepped out of the truck. "Looks like I got here just in time," he said. "You two were getting the hard end of that fight."

"We could've taken them," Joe replied.

Frank rubbed the side of his face. "We were getting our clocks cleaned, Joe."

"Speak for yourself."

The other racer asked Joe what the fight was about.

Joe had some ideas, but he didn't think it was a good idea to share them with just anyone. "Don't know," he said. "Maybe they wanted my sled."

The Hardys helped the pickup driver load his own snowmobile up on its trailer, then got in the van and started home.

Cold air rushed in the broken side window as they drove.

"One of those guys had an ice ax," Frank said. "The other one had a snowmobile track."

"And they both wore snocross helmets."

Frank nodded. "That means it probably was Rick Salazar and Jim Edwards."

"The only question is, why?" Joe observed. "Salazar probably did try to take you out on the ice wall, and Edwards played rough in the snocross, but it's over now. Edwards has no reason to be after me anymore."

Frank told Joe about his attacker saying something about Neal Jordan.

Joe rubbed his chin. "Maybe Fred Vale put them up to it. He was hoping for a big blowup between me and Jim."

"That's pretty far-fetched, Joe. Those two guys were trying to put us out of commission permanently. Imagine the headlines: 'Two Athletes Killed After Snocross Race.' That kind of publicity would ruin Vale and the Max Games."

Joe had to agree.

When they got home, Frank taped a piece of plastic over the broken window before they headed inside.

Joe found a note on the kitchen table. "Mom and Dad are out," he told Frank. "They say congratulations. They saw my race on TV and they'll be at the medal ceremony tonight. Dinner's in the oven."

They sat down to plates of delicious hot roast beef, carrots, and garlic bread.

"I've got a plan," Frank said as he ladled gravy over his meat.

"Let's hear it."

"Most of the athletes are staying at the Atlantic Bay Hotel, right?"

Joe took a swig of milk. "It's the only place big enough."

"While you and Jim Edwards are at the stadium getting your medals tonight, I'll sneak into the hotel to see if I can get into his room. Maybe we'll get some clue about what he and Salazar are up to."

"Sounds good," Joe said, his mouth full of bread.

At a little after eight o'clock, Joe killed the van's lights and pulled into the service drive behind the Atlantic Bay Hotel. He stopped at the employees' entrance.

Frank was wearing black slacks and a white dress shirt. "How do I look?" he asked, adjusting his narrow black tie.

"Like you're ready to take my dinner order," Joe said, with a laugh.

Frank did a mock bow. "I'm here to serve you, sir." Then he jumped out of the van. "See you in an hour or so."

When Joe was gone, Frank walked into the hotel, acting as though he belonged there.

A wide, well-lit hallway led past the employee locker room. He passed through a pair of swinging doors to his right and found himself in the kitchen. It bustled with activity. A chef worked over a huge gas stove, tossing some kind of vegetables around in a skillet. Other people were busy washing dishes and adding garnishes to great-looking desserts.

Frank kept his head down and walked fast. He went through a door at the far end of the kitchen and found himself in a little alcove with a cash register and a coffee machine. It was the wait station, where servers calculated the customers' bills and punched in orders.

Frank turned toward the wall as a waitress hustled past. "Can you pick up some clean napkins?" she asked.

Frank held his hand up to shield his face. "Sure. No problem," he said.

When she disappeared into the kitchen, he checked for a phone where guests would call in room-service orders. There it was, on the wall next to the cash register.

As he'd hoped, he found a stack of room-service orders stuck to a spike on the counter.

Frank flipped through them quickly. Some had no names on them, just the room number and the order. He was looking for Jim Edwards's room, when he passed a familiar name. He flipped back through the last couple of receipts. There it was: R. Salazar—Rm. 506.

Yes! Frank said to himself. Quickly, he grabbed a tray and some stainless steel dish covers from shelves under the counter. Now he looked like a real waiter.

Carrying the tray on his shoulder, he strode to the service elevator. He was up on the fifth floor in no time.

He stepped off the elevator cautiously. He peered down the hall in both directions. It was totally quiet. Frank headed to his right, stopping in front of room 506. He knocked on the door. "Room service."

He figured he'd act as if it was a big joke if Salazar came to the door.

No one answered.

Setting down the tray, Frank pulled lock picks out of his wallet and went to work. The door opened easily. He was in.

He flipped on the lights. The room was neat—the bed was made, and no open bags were in sight.

Coiled on the cushion of an overstuffed chair was a length of climbing rope. Frank ran it through his hands. It was the exact same kind as the one that was in the safety harness at the ice wall. Frank touched a frayed end with his thumb. It looked as if it had been cut, and he thought that it might be the rope from the ice wall. Again, there was no way to be sure.

He went to the desk. Now what are these? he asked himself, picking up a stack of maps. There was a road map of the state of New York. Frank unfolded it. He didn't see anything unusual about it.

The other maps were more interesting, though. There were no roads on them. They looked like pools of blue water, with waves running out from the center.

"Topographical maps," Frank whispered aloud, "used for surveying and hiking." The maps were all of the Catskill Mountains and showed the elevation and details of the terrain.

What would Salazar need these for? Frank wondered.

He went over to the closet and opened it. Here was something interesting!

He reached in and pulled out a heavy target air rifle. The kind they use in the maximum biathlon, Frank noted. The only problem was that Salazar wasn't entered in the biathlon.

He turned the gun over in his hands. It was obviously almost new. The wooden stock was carefully oiled, and the blued barrel was polished to a bright shine.

Putting the rifle back, he checked the closet shelf. He pulled down a wooden case about the size of a cigar box.

Opening it, he saw two neat rows of tiny feathered darts. They looked as though they would fit the gun.

Frank was putting the case back when he heard voices approaching from out in the hall.

He froze. "Go away, go on past," he whispered to himself.

The voices grew louder. Then Frank heard the sound of a key sliding into a lock.

They were coming in.

10 Break-in

At the stadium Joe stood on the running track with Jim Edwards and the third-place finisher in the snocross, Omar Korrel.

Fred Vale frantically adjusted the camera angles. He kept moving the three athletes closer together, as if that might prompt an outburst from Joe or Jim.

For his part, Joe stayed quiet. He watched Jim closely though, looking for any clue or sign that he'd been one of the guys who'd attacked the Hardys earlier that evening.

Joe was scanning the crowd for his parents when Jim tapped him on the shoulder.

"Look, Joe," Edwards said quietly. "I'm sorry about being a sore loser earlier. You had a great race."

This caught Joe by surprise. He hadn't expected Edwards to be nice.

"I guess I've been pretty angry lately about losing my sponsor," Jim continued. "I took it out on you." He held out his hand to shake.

Joe took it.

"I've gotten a rap as a dangerous driver," Edwards admitted. "That's what cost me my sponsorship."

"You don't think you're dangerous?"

Jim looked away. "I thought I was just doing whatever it took to win. Then I crossed the line and started playing dirty. I'm going to change that, though."

"You'll win again soon," Joe replied.

When Vale saw them, his jaw dropped. "What? You two are best buddies now?"

Joe and Jim smiled at the camera. Vale seemed disappointed, but the ceremony went off without a hitch.

Joe lifted the heavy gold medal off his chest and held it out for the crowd to see. The cheers were deafening, and the exploding flashes left colored spots in front of Joe's eyes.

Swiftly Frank replaced the box of darts and closed the closet door.

The key turned in the lock.

Frank dashed to the bed and dropped to the

floor. Too low! There was no way he could fit under the bed frame.

As the door opened, Frank darted into the bathroom. He climbed into the shower and silently closed the curtain.

He recognized the voices of Rick Salazar and Amanda Mollica out in the main room.

"I want to know why he's acting this way," Mollica was saying, concern in her voice.

"What do you mean?" Salazar asked. "He always tries to steal the show."

"But this is different. These are incredible chances he's taking. He opened his chute so late at the opening ceremony that I thought he was going to die."

Salazar sounded impatient. "Amanda, you don't have to hang with us anymore if you're going to wig out like this."

"I'm just asking what's going on."

"It's all part of a plan," Salazar answered. Frank heard him pull something out of a dresser drawer.

"This is gonna be the greatest stunt anyone ever pulled off," Salazar continued. "But we don't need you if you're not up for it."

Then they left the room, and Frank couldn't make out Mollica's reply.

Frank eased out of the shower cautiously. In only a few more seconds, he could complete the search. Going to the dresser, he opened each drawer in turn. Salazar's clothes, his ice axes—nothing unusual about them—a headset walkie-talkie.

A headset walkie-talkie? Frank lifted the specially designed, lightweight radio from the drawer. It was the kind sky divers used to communicate with each other in midair. A plastic earpiece allowed you to talk without using your hands to touch anything. Why would Salazar need one? He didn't skydive.

Frank put the radio back where he found it, then looked at his watch. There was time to check one or two more rooms before Joe would arrive to pick him up.

He opened the door a crack. The hall was clear. Stepping out, he noticed the room-service tray he'd left outside the door. He wiped his forehead in an exaggerated gesture of relief. He couldn't believe Salazar hadn't noticed the tray and suspected something.

With his foot, he slid the tray down the hall a few feet. Now no one could be sure which room it belonged to.

If Salazar, Sammy Fear, and Jim Edwards were all in on something, Frank wondered, wouldn't they want their rooms to be close together?

He knocked on the room across the hall. No answer. He jimmied the lock and stepped inside. In the closet, Frank found a neat row of business suits. This was obviously not the room of a Max Games athlete. He slipped out.

When he put his ear to the door to the left of Salazar's room, Frank heard the television yapping away. He moved on to the next room down.

This one was also empty. He went in and immediately knew he'd found Jim Edwards's room. Clothes were strewn all over. Edwards's bright green racing suit was draped over the desk chair, and snowmobile parts littered the bed and floor.

He sifted through a stack of papers on the desk. Edwards had three letters from snowmobile companies. Each one said almost exactly the same thing: if Edwards won the Max Games they would seriously consider sponsoring him in the future.

At the bottom of the pile, he found another interesting letter. It read:

Dear Justice:

I'm pleased to hear you'll be competing in the Max Games snocross event. I'm aware that you usually receive a five-thousand-dollar fee to appear at such events.

Unfortunately, due to financial limitations, I can't pay you to be here. However, I can offer you great television exposure and a chance to attract top sponsors.

I hope you'll still be able to compete.

The letter was signed by Fred Vale.

Frank felt a chill go down his spine. Here was evidence that Vale was having money problems.

Could that be the reason for all the wild stuff going on?

Frank tossed the letters down and went over to the phone. There he found a yellow sticky pad with a short note on it: "Talk to Fear again about quick $." Frank remembered seeing Fear and Edwards together in the pit area after Joe's first wreck. What were they in on?

Frank made one last search of the room. The one thing he didn't find was a spare snowmobile track like the one the thug had used to smash his face just a couple of hours earlier. But of course that could still be at the stadium. Frank hoped Joe hadn't run into trouble.

He needn't have worried. By the time he'd retraced his steps and escaped unnoticed out the hotel service door, Joe was waiting for him.

Frank jumped in the van and pulled off his tie.

"That thing strangling you?" Joe joked.

"Like a rope," Frank said, tossing the offending garment into the back of the van. "How'd the ceremony go?"

Joe flashed his gold medal. "Nice, huh?"

Frank studied it. Almost the size of a hockey puck, the medal showed a snowmobile and rider flying through the air. Around the edge, lettering said, Third Annual Max Games Snocross Champion. "Beautiful," Frank said. "I can't wait till I win one for ice climbing tomorrow."

Joe wheeled the van through the quiet streets. "Find anything in the hotel?"

"I think I got some good clues." Frank told Joe about what he'd found and the conversation between Mollica and Salazar.

"What could the big stunt be?" Joe asked, mostly to himself.

"Don't know," Frank replied. "But I thought it was pretty strange that Salazar had a target rifle and a skydiving radio."

"Fred Vale must be behind it all," Joe said. "That letter just about proves he'll go broke unless the Max Games do great this year."

Frank stared out the window for a moment, thinking. "How did Edwards act at the awards?"

"Totally cool," Joe answered. "I'm starting to change my mind about him. He seems like a good guy."

"Don't make friends too quickly," Frank warned. "I figure he's involved in all this somehow."

Both Hardys were exhausted by the time they pulled into the driveway. They talked to their parents for a few minutes—Frank tried to explain his swollen face—then went upstairs to go to sleep.

Joe bolted upright in bed. His clock radio read 5:15 A.M. He listened intently. A car hummed by, its lights making his curtains glow for a second.

There! He heard it again. A sound from outside.

He got up, slipped on some sneakers, and padded over to Frank's room.

"Frank. Wake up," he whispered.

"What? Huh?" Frank rolled over.

Joe heard the noise again. A clunk, like something metallic hitting the driveway. He went over to Frank's window and peered out. There was the van, right where he'd parked it. He could see the small hole the ice ax had made in the roof.

He heard the noise again, and the van seemed to rock a little—or was it his imagination?

Now Frank was fully awake.

Joe held a finger to his lips, motioning for his brother to stay quiet. Together they crept downstairs and outside, where it was cold and dark.

Joe edged silently around the back of the van. At first he didn't see anything unusual. Then his eyes adjusted to the darkness.

He motioned for Frank to take a look.

Frank followed Joe's gaze. The side door of the van was open, and someone was inside.

11 A Cold Contest

The Hardys crept forward, Frank leading the way. Staying close to the side of the van, Frank leaned over and peeked in the open door. He saw something move and pulled his head back quickly.

"One guy, I think," he whispered to Joe.

"I say we rush him."

Frank nodded. He sprang in front of the door, only to get hit in the mouth with a long-barreled flashlight.

Joe saw his brother crumple to the ground in pain. A figure dressed all in black, his face covered with a ski mask, jumped from the van.

The guy sprinted past Joe toward the street.

"Get him!" Frank shouted.

Joe took off down the driveway. With his running

back's speed, he figured he'd catch this joker in no time.

Frank's assailant had other plans, though. He cut across the Hardys' front lawn.

Joe saw what the guy was running for: there was a mountain bike leaning against the Hardys' mailbox post.

The two of them were going full speed when they made it to the street. As Joe was about to make a diving tackle, he felt his foot go out from under him. He'd slipped on a patch of ice. He went down hard, cracking his elbow on the pavement and yowling in pain.

Joe tried to stand up. If he could knock the guy off the bike, he and Frank could get some answers.

But what he saw sent a rush of fear and adrenaline through his body.

The bike speeding toward him had steel-studded ice tires. They'd shred his skin like razor blades.

His attacker pedaled furiously.

Joe dove toward the curb. The front tire of the bike clipped his right heel, and then the rider was gone into the darkness.

Joe sat up and caught his breath. His right shoe had a two-inch rip in it, but he was unhurt.

He got up to check on his brother. Frank was inside the van, rummaging around. His lip was swollen and bloody, and his face was a kaleidoscope of colors from the attack the night before, but other than that he was okay.

"Nothing seems to be missing," he said.

Joe rubbed his arms to keep warm. "We must've scared him off before he could find whatever he was after."

Frank nodded. "Did you see who it was?"

"Had a ski mask on," Joe said. "But I'd bet the fact that he was riding a mountain bike with mean-looking ice tires means he's connected to the Max Games somehow."

The Hardys heard their mother's voice. "What's going on out there, you two?"

Frank slammed the van door shut. "Let's get some breakfast."

Laura Hardy gasped when she saw Frank's newest injury. "What happened now?" She got some ice for his swollen lip from the freezer.

"Somebody broke into the van," Joe said. "We chased him off."

Mrs. Hardy handed Frank the ice. "Should I wake your father? Or call the police?"

Frank shook his head. "The guy didn't get away with anything valuable."

"And if I find out who it was, he's not going to get away with clocking you in the face."

"Joe," Mrs. Hardy scolded. "Sit down. Since we're all up, I'll make some pancakes."

Several hours later, the Hardys met Jamal outside the athletes' entrance to the climbing wall.

"You juiced, Frank?"

Frank knocked fists with Jamal. "You got it, man. Big day today—ice climb, then sky surfing."

"What happened to your face?"

"He tried to stop a truck with it," Joe quipped.

Frank punched his brother in the shoulder, then started to fill Jamal in on everything that had happened since the previous night.

As they walked to the benches around the wall, Frank spotted Mollica, Fear, and Salazar and had to clam up. "I'll tell you more later," he whispered.

Jamal nodded. They set their climbing gear down on the bench right next to Salazar's.

One official was busy checking the hardness of the ice, while another started and stopped the electronic clock over and over again, making certain it worked perfectly.

Frank glanced up at the sky. Clear, not too cold. It was going to be a beautiful day.

Rick Salazar ruined Frank's mood by pestering him about his near fall the day before. "Hey, Frank," he called. "You bring your parachute today?"

"Don't humiliate Frank too much today," Fear said, sitting on the bench next to Rick. "Amanda and I want something to be left for us to destroy in the sky-surfing competition."

"I'm ready for anything you've got, Sammy. You, too, Rick," Frank said.

Fear grinned. "We'll see, won't we?"

"Yo, Sammy!" someone called.

They all turned to see Jim Edwards show his athlete's ID and come through the gate.

"Sammy," he said. "You ready now?"

"Yeah," Fear called. He gave Frank a hard stare as he walked past. Frank didn't blink.

"You could break that dude in two," Jamal said as Edwards and Fear headed back toward the stadium.

Joe leaned close to his brother. "I'm going to follow those two. See what's up."

"Good idea."

"Yo, ladies!" Salazar chided. "No telling secrets. It's rude."

Joe laughed him off. "No big secret, man. Just going to the stadium to get a snack."

Joe hurried after Edwards and Fear, staying far enough back so they wouldn't notice him.

To Joe's surprise, the two athletes ended up in the snocross pit area. Though he was too far away to hear what they were saying to each other, it was obvious that Edwards was teaching Fear some basic snocross riding techniques.

Fear straddled Jim's sled. As Edwards talked to him, he leaned left, then right, then stood up on the side runners.

After about ten minutes of this, Jim started up the snowmobile and coasted it slowly onto the track. He then stepped back and watched as Sammy got on and took off slowly around the course.

Joe was startled to hear someone call his name.

He turned toward the voice. Edwards was waving to him.

"Joe! Come on over and watch this."

Joe realized he'd have to make up a story quickly or either Edwards or Fear would figure out that he'd been following them. He ambled over to Jim.

"How come you're not at the ice wall, watching your brother?" Edwards asked.

"Oh, the competition hasn't started yet," Joe replied. "And I wanted to get one last thing cleared up between us."

Jim looked at him suspiciously. "Yeah, what?"

"That replacement ski you gave me for my sled. How come it broke?"

Jim laughed. "I didn't sabotage it, if that's what you're wondering."

Joe blushed. "I had to ask."

"Since I lost my sponsor, I've had to buy cheap parts," Jim said. "It just gave out on you, that's all."

Joe nodded.

Jim pointed to Sammy, who was now bounding around the course at a good pace. "Can you believe that nut? He's paying me to give him snocross lessons. Claims he's going to start competing in the maximum biathlon."

Joe watched Sammy go around and around. He believed Edwards about the broken ski. He even believed that the lessons he was now giving Fear explained the note Frank had found in his hotel room. But there was one other question—and it was a big one. Who were the guys who'd come after them with an ice ax and a snowmobile track the previous evening?

"Speaking of spare parts," Joe said as casually as he could, "someone broke into our van this morning. I don't know what they were looking for."

"No way!" Edwards said. "That happened to me, too. Some jerk snatched the only spare track I had for my sled. If I find the guy, he's dead."

"Not if I catch him first," Joe said with a smile.

Joe believed Jim was telling the truth. That meant he wasn't one of the two thugs he and Frank had gone up against.

He told Jim he'd catch him later and headed over to the ice wall.

By the time he made it back, the competition had already started. The stands were filling up, and the top five climbing times were posted on the electronic scoreboard.

He sat down next to Frank. "How's it going?"

"The wall is tough," Frank said. "A few guys haven't even been able to finish it." He pointed to the wall. "You're just in time, though. Jamal's up."

"Who's he paired with?" Joe asked. He knew that ice climbers didn't race against each other as much as they raced against the clock. Though it helped to be paired with someone who would push you to climb your best, beating him wasn't worth much if your time was slow. The three fastest times would get medals. That was it.

"Dirk Polking," Frank replied. "It'll be a good race."

The starter's gun fired. Joe watched as Jamal and Dirk scrambled to the wall and started up.

They were even until Polking slipped. He dropped a few feet before the safety line stopped his fall. He hung there by his harness, spinning slowly.

"All right, Jamal!" Frank shouted as Jamal reached the top and slapped the timer with one palm.

Max Games officials then used the safety lines to lower both Jamal and Dirk back to earth.

They switched sides, and the starter pulled the trigger again.

This time Dirk didn't fall. He slapped the timer just a few hundredths of a second behind Jamal, but it didn't matter; his failure on the first climb had cost him any chance at a medal.

Joe pointed at the scoreboard. "Take a look, Frank. Jamal's in first place."

"Awesome!"

Frank didn't have time to congratulate his friend. The next two names the announcer called were Hardy and Salazar.

12 The Hunch

Frank could feel Rick staring at him as they walked to the wall and strapped on the safety harnesses. "You're gonna lose, Hardy," Salazar hissed. "I'm going to humiliate you in front of all these people."

Frank ignored him. Looking up the steep sheet of ice, he tried to pick the fastest line to the top. He watched as a huge, silver blimp passed overhead, flashing ads for a popular soft drink.

Frank hefted his ice axes. He was ready.

The starter's gun went off, and Frank began his climb up the wall.

His crampons dug into the ice with a crunch. Shards of glistening ice rained down on his head with each blow of his ice axes.

The muscles in his arms started to burn, but the

frenzied cheering of the crowd made him climb even harder.

He thought he could hear Salazar's axes biting into the wall just a few feet away. How high was he? Frank didn't dare look over.

He reached up and slammed his fist into the timer, then let go of the wall, allowing the safety rope to catch his fall.

As he gasped for breath, the crowd screamed its approval. From among the voices, Frank heard his brother shout, "Way to go, Frank!"

He looked at the clock. He was in the lead!

As the crew lowered them to the group, Salazar called over, "You got lucky, man. Now we'll see how you do on the hard side."

"If you climbed as well as you talked, you'd be winning," Frank retorted.

When they reached the ground, they took off their safety harnesses to switch sides. As they walked past each other, Salazar lashed out at Frank's leg with his crampon spikes.

Frank tried to jump back but felt the sharp metal tear into his left shin. A few people in the crowd cried out angrily. The officials, however, didn't see the cheap shot.

Frank felt blood trickling down into his boot, but he didn't even have time to check the injury—the officials were calling for the two athletes to get ready for the second climb.

Frank's leg throbbed. He thought of telling an

official but dismissed the idea. This was between the two of them. He glared at Rick, getting only a smug grin in return.

The second heat started.

Frank climbed on guts alone. Twice his leg gave out on him as he scrambled up the ice, and those slips cost him precious time.

He slapped the timer.

Frank knew he'd lost before he even looked at the clock. Salazar was lying back in his harness, arms outstretched in celebration as officials lowered him to the ground.

Without even shaking hands with Frank, Salazar dropped his harness and started jumping up and down.

Frank looked at the clock. Salazar had won the gold. Jamal was second, and Frank had ended up third.

Joe and Jamal came running up to him. "Frank, you've got to file a protest, man. We saw what happened," Jamal said.

"I'm going to wipe that smile off his face," Joe said.

Frank grabbed his brother by the arm. "Let it go. It's over, bro. And we've got to start getting ready for the sky surfing."

Frank congratulated Jamal on his silver medal.

"Thanks, Frank. You and Joe have had some really bad luck lately."

Frank nodded. "Almost falling off the ice wall,

the two guys who attacked us, Joe's wipeouts. I don't think it's bad luck. Somebody wants us out of the Max Games—permanently. But who? Salazar, Fear, Edwards?"

"And why?" Joe added.

A camera crew tried to get an interview, but Frank waved them off. He sat on a bench and pulled up the cuff of his pants. An ugly two-inch gash still oozed blood.

Jamal dug antiseptic, a gauze pad, and some tape from his bag. "I always keep this stuff around for blisters," he said. "Wrap up that cut, man. It's nasty."

"I don't think Edwards is in on it," Joe said quietly. He told Frank and Jamal about the conversation he'd had with Jim earlier. "He was over there showing Sammy Fear how to ride a snowmobile."

"Sky surfing's the last event," Frank said, tending to his leg. "If Sammy has some dangerous stunt planned, it's going to happen soon." He looked up at his two sky-surfing partners. "Keep your eyes open, guys. Be ready for anything."

Both Joe and Jamal nodded gravely.

It was late morning when the Hardys stepped out of the Hawkins Air Service building onto the asphalt runway.

They watched Jamal taxi the single-engine plane out of the hangar and steer it toward them.

111

When Jamal stopped, Joe jogged up to the plane and opened the passenger door. He and Frank tossed their chutes inside.

Jamal stepped out of the plane. "Something weird's going on," he said to Frank and Joe. He threw a glance over to the hangar, where four other small planes sat lined up and ready to go. "Sammy Fear just told my dad that he wouldn't need a pilot for his plane."

"What? He hired his own pilot?" Frank asked. He looked over. Sky-surfing contestants milled around the hangar or stood next to the planes, putting on their colorful jumpsuits. He didn't see Sammy Fear or Amanda Mollica.

"I guess so," Jamal replied. "Games officials were a little upset about it—they don't like last-minute changes—but they said it was okay."

Frank smiled. "The question is, how does your dad feel about someone he doesn't know flying one of his planes?"

"He's dealing with it," Jamal said, laughing.

Joe checked his helmet cam. "What's the jump order?"

"We're in the first group," Jamal said, pulling a sheet of paper out of his pocket and unfolding it. "The Max Games are so big we're putting five planes in the air at once. After a team jumps, the pilot has to come back here to pick up the next team."

Frank zipped up his bright red jumpsuit. "How about Fear and Mollica?"

"They go right before you guys."

Joe pointed at the hangar. "There they are."

The three friends watched as Sammy Fear, his long hair hanging out under his helmet, climbed into one of the planes.

"That's Amanda with him, of course," Jamal said. "But who's the pilot?"

The third figure getting in wore sunglasses and a ski cap pulled down low against the wind. "I can't tell," Frank said.

"Sammy just wants any edge he can get in the competition," Joe said. "If he feels better with his own pilot, who cares. We'll still beat them."

"That's right," Jamal said. "The gold is ours."

When officials were satisfied they had everything organized, the five airplanes, loaded with the first five teams, took off into the air and headed toward the stadium.

Jamal climbed to ten thousand feet.

Joe gazed out his window. At this height he could see the entire city of Bayport. Each city block was the size of a postage stamp. "You've got thirty seconds to show your stuff, Frank. You ready?"

Frank was busy clamping his boots into the bindings on his sky surfboard. "Ready," Frank replied. "Just follow the plan."

The Hardys had rehearsed their aerobatics for

months. Frank would execute his spins, flips, and flying positions precisely. It was Joe's job to get it all on camera artistically so the crowd and judges could see the incredible show on the Jumbotron in the stadium.

As Joe put on his parachute and cinched it tight, he heard Jamal speaking rapidly into the radio up in the cockpit. "Everything cool?" he asked.

Jamal looked back over his shoulder. "Sammy Fear's up to something," he called over the drone of the engine.

Frank and Joe looked at each other.

"Fear and Mollica didn't jump," Jamal continued.

"What happened?" Frank asked. "Is something wrong with their plane?"

"No. They didn't head back to the airport," Jamal replied. "They took off due west. The tower's trying to contact them, but they won't answer."

Joe held up his hands in a gesture of futility. "The guy's crazy. Who knows what he's up to."

"They want you guys to go ahead and jump," Jamal said. "I'll bring the plane around, then you can open the door."

Putting on their helmets and goggles, the Hardys got ready to jump.

"Ten seconds," Jamal said. Then he started counting down.

Frank opened the door, and the cold wind came howling in.

"Seven, six, five—" Jamal said.

Frank slammed the door shut and ripped off his goggles. "Jamal! Head west," he shouted.

"What're you doing, Frank?"

Frank looked at his brother, then motioned for him to sit down again. "I think I figured out what Fear's big stunt is," he said. "They're going to kidnap Neal Jordan."

"What?" Jamal shouted. "That's nuts!"

"No, listen," Frank said. "It all makes sense." He held out his hand and ticked off one finger with each fact. "The maps of the Catskill Mountains I found in Salazar's hotel room; the sky-diving radio; that wild stunt when Fear and Mollica BASE-jumped from the stadium and Salazar rappelled down—that was practice for the kidnapping attempt. They're going to fly over the presidential retreat, skydive, and somehow grab Neal."

Joe stared at his brother in disbelief.

"They already tried to kidnap Neal once," Frank said. "At the snowboard aerials yesterday."

Joe's expression changed. "You mean that prank Sammy pulled by taking Neal's jump for him?"

"He told Neal to meet Amanda over at the stadium. That proves it wasn't a spur-of-the-moment thing like Sammy said. He had a plan, but Agent DuBelle and I screwed it up."

"And this is their backup plan," Joe said.

Frank nodded. He dug his wallet out of his pack and found a phone number Neal had given him to

115

call when they were ready to visit him in the Catskills.

Going to the cockpit, he sat down in the copilot's seat, next to Jamal. "Get on the radio," he said. "Get us patched in to this number."

Less than a minute later, Frank was talking to Agent Ardis at the presidential retreat.

"That sounds pretty far-fetched," Ardis said. "I think you should stick to sky surfing and let the Secret Service do its job, young man."

"Just be extra careful," Frank said.

"I'll put everyone on alert," Ardis replied, but Frank could tell by the tone of his voice that the agent was only humoring him.

Then Neal got on the line. "Frank, man?"

"Yeah."

"Dude, the skiing's great."

"Excellent!" Frank said. "We'll be there in about—" He looked at Jamal.

"Thirty, maybe thirty-five minutes," Jamal said.

Frank relayed the information to Neal and signed off.

About half an hour later, Jamal pointed out of the windshield. "There's the lodge," he reported.

"Circle around," Frank said.

Jamal took the plane around, while Frank studied the horizon. There was no sign of another airplane. Maybe he'd been wrong about Sammy Fear's plans after all.

116

As Jamal took the plane up to five thousand feet, a safe skydiving altitude, Frank and Joe got ready to jump.

Joe opened the door and looked out. "This is a pretty intense way to drop in for a visit," he said.

Frank laughed as he pulled down his goggles. "See you on the ground," he said, and jumped out into the wind.

Seconds later Joe followed.

The wind grabbed him for a second as he cleared the plane, then he was falling free and clear.

He enjoyed the view as he counted off the seconds. The mountains were beautiful, and the snow was so white in the bright sun that it made his eyes hurt.

He pulled his rip cord.

From experience, Joe expected the chute to jerk him up as it opened and caught air. He felt a slight tug—that was all.

Joe heard a ripping sound and looked up. His heart caught in his throat.

His main chute and his reserve had come out in one big tangled ball. The wind whipped at the knotted mass over his head.

He was not slowing down.

13 Free Fall

Joe realized that the guy who had broken into the van hadn't wanted to steal anything—he'd wanted to sabotage the chutes!

He spun so fast now that his vision was a blur of flashes of blue sky, then dark earth. It all seemed to blend together.

Frank saw the trouble his brother was in, but he'd already opened his chute. There was no way he could dive down to help. He watched in shock as Joe fell like a stone, growing smaller and smaller in the distance.

Joe was falling so fast now that he saw black spots in front of his eyes—he was about to lose consciousness. He had to do something, anything.

Digging into the pocket of his jumpsuit, he found his pocketknife.

The freezing wind tore at the knife, trying to rip it from his cold fingers. He got the blade open and reached overhead to the tangle of cords.

Blindly he started cutting. The blade went through the cords one and two at a time. Joe had no idea if he was cutting lines to the reserve or the main chute. He only knew he was going to hit the ground any second now.

He sliced through another cord. He felt something give way. Looking up, Joe saw his reserve chute rip away.

The main chute unfurled about halfway—three or four of its cords were gone. Joe thought he was slowing down a little. But was it too little, too late?

He gasped in pain as something slammed into his ribs like a baseball bat.

Realizing he'd hit a tree, Joe reached out to try to grab a branch—anything to slow himself down a little.

He tumbled through the branches in a cold cloud of snow and snapping limbs.

He slammed into the ground, and all the whiteness of the snow suddenly went black.

Frank had watched helplessly as Joe disappeared into the top of a tall, snow-laden pine tree. His only thought as he fell was, How am I going to tell Mom and Dad that Joe is dead?

119

Frantically, his heart trying to pound its way out of his chest, Frank steered his chute in the direction of the pine tree.

He landed softly and cut his chute. He had to get to Joe.

He found his brother facedown, spread-eagle in a snowdrift. "Joe!" he yelled, dropping to his knees next to the body.

Joe lifted his head slowly. Snow plugged his nose and stuck to his eyebrows. "Am I alive?" he asked.

Frank was so relieved he laughed. "Yeah, you're alive."

"Good, 'cause I sure don't feel alive." Joe spit out some snow, rolled over, and sat up. He released the few remaining lines to his chute. "Good thing I hit that tree."

"You made an excellent snow angel," Frank quipped. "But I thought you were going to be playing a harp, bro."

"So did I."

Several people came running across the field to the Hardys.

Frank saw that one of them was Neal Jordan. "We saw it all!" Neal shouted breathlessly. "Joe, are you alive?"

"We were just discussing that," Joe replied.

Neal laughed. "That was some entrance, dude! Sammy Fear's got nothing on you."

Agent Ardis and a couple of other agents helped

Joe to his feet. As they walked to the lodge, Ardis let the Hardys know he was angry.

"Why couldn't you two land at the airport and get a ride out here like normal people?" he asked. "Or we could've had someone pick you up there."

"The nearest airport is forty miles away," Frank said. "And we were worried about what Sammy Fear might be up to."

Ardis shook his head. "He's not up to anything. This is all absurd."

Frank bit his tongue. He didn't want to get into an argument. And besides, he wasn't positive that Neal was in any danger. After all, it would be foolish for anyone to think they could get away with kidnapping the president's son.

An armed agent let them through an eight-foot iron gate. The retreat was a huge log house nestled high on the side of a mountain. There was a concrete helipad out front, and several black sport-utes were parked along a drive leading up to the side of the house.

"Wow!" Joe said. "There must be room for twenty or thirty people to stay here, and the view is great."

"Yup," Neal said. "My dad has guests up here a lot. And there has to be room for these guys," he added, nodding at the agents.

Another agent let them in the front door. Inside, a fire crackled warmly at the far end of a long living room.

Agent DuBelle greeted the Hardys with a concerned but friendly smile. "Agent Ardis radioed me about your accident," she said. "It's amazing you're not hurt."

Joe agreed. They all sat down around a square coffee table in front of the fire. A tray of hot soup and sandwiches appeared only a few seconds later. The Hardys and Neal dug in.

"It wasn't an accident," Joe said. He and Frank related the story of the guy breaking into their van. "We must have caught him before he could get to Frank's chute."

"How do you know that?" Ardis said. "Your chute could have malfunctioned on its own."

"I doubt it," Joe said.

"Yeah," Frank added. "These are the newest chutes, and Joe's an expert packer."

DuBelle stood up and went over to the fire. "It's too much of a coincidence that someone broke into your van, and then your chute malfunctioned."

"Right," Frank said. "That means the guy knew about parachutes."

"Sammy Fear," Neal said.

Agent Ardis sighed loudly. "This is silly speculation."

DuBelle shook her head. "I think we need to be cautious."

Ardis threw his arms up in exasperation. "Okay, fine. We'll all be careful. But Sammy Fear's plane left the airport before the Hardys' plane, and there's no sign of him anywhere."

No one could answer that one.

"It's a perfect afternoon," Ardis said to Neal. "Why don't you kids let us worry about Sammy Fear? Neal, take your friends out on the slopes for some snowboarding."

Neal grinned. "Sounds good to me."

"The only problem is, we didn't bring our stuff," Frank said. "We didn't plan to arrive this way."

"That's okay," Neal said. He led the Hardys over to a big storage closet in an alcove off the kitchen. He opened the door. It looked like a ski shop inside. Rows of boots and skis lined the walls. "Like I said, there are a few benefits to being the son of the president. When important guests show up, we don't want them to have to worry about anything."

The Hardys picked out boots that fit, while Neal rummaged around for two of his spare snowboards.

Within minutes Neal, the Hardys, and four agents, including Ardis and DuBelle, were heading outside to hit the slopes.

They hiked a few hundred yards away from the lodge to the start of a nice, steep slope that cut between tall rows of pine and spruce trees. Neal pointed down the mountain. "It's pretty fast," he said. "Follow my lead the first time down."

"There's no ski lift," Joe said. "Are we going to hike back up?"

Neal laughed. "No way." He pointed back toward the house. Three agents came roaring out of a storage garage on snowmobiles. "They'll follow us down and give us a lift back up."

"This is the life," Frank said as he clipped into his board and took off down the mountain after Neal.

The snow was fresh, perfect powder, and the three teens cut down the mountain quickly, dodging between trees and popping over small jumps.

When they reached the bottom, the agents were waiting to take them up.

At the top of the run, they huddled together. The agents on snowmobiles idled their engines nearby. "You guys know the hill now?" Neal asked.

Joe nodded enthusiastically. "Let's race, man. Free-for-all!"

"Hold up, Joe!" Frank hurried to clip back into his board. As he bent down, he thought he heard the drone of an airplane in the distance. He looked up and scanned the sky. Nothing. He must have imagined it.

Then two of the agents slumped over the handlebars of their snowmobiles. The third tumbled off his and lay in the snow.

Frank saw a look of confusion and fear on Neal's face. What was going on?

124

Frank looked up again. Two parachutists were dropping out of the sky overhead. One pointed a rifle at Frank. The gun made a sinister, hissing pop, and Frank dove behind a tree.

He peeked out. All the agents were down, including Ardis and DuBelle.

Neal stood out in the open, frozen with fear.

14 Silent Attack

"Neal! Joe!" Frank shouted. "Dive for cover!"

Frank watched as his brother took a step toward Neal to pull him to safety. Joe stopped, grabbed at his leg, then stumbled and fell to his knees.

He'd been hit!

The two parachutists released their chutes expertly as they swooped in to land. One ran over and pulled the agents clear from the snowmobiles. The other grabbed Neal.

Frank wasn't about to let them get away—guns or not. With a wild yell, he rushed out from behind the tree, head lowered.

He felt a projectile whiz past his ear. He dove for the gunman, his hands reaching for the barrel of the rifle.

126

Pain shot through the back of his skull. Frank collapsed in the snow.

He had to get up. He made it to one knee. Everything was spinning. He thought he might throw up.

Frank shook his head to clear the cobwebs. By the time his vision cleared, the two kidnappers had Neal and were roaring off on the snowmobiles.

He looked around. Everyone else was down. Only Joe moved at all. He was trying to sit up but kept falling back.

Frank took a handful of snow and rubbed it over his face to help himself wake up—the guy must have clubbed him on the head with the rifle stock.

He got to Joe.

"Where are you hit?"

"The, ah, leg," Joe said slowly.

Frank checked him out. There, sticking out of Joe's thigh, was a plumed dart exactly like the one Frank had seen in Salazar's hotel room. So, he thought. Rick Salazar was the third person who got on the plane with Amanda and Sammy today. That meant Salazar and Fear were the kidnappers. And that they were probably the guys who'd attacked the Hardys with the ice ax and the sled track.

Frank pulled out the dart and smelled the tip. It smelled like the animal tranquilizer he'd seen his friend Chet use when he worked at the zoo.

Luckily, Joe's snowsuit had kept the dart from

penetrating too far. He was groggy, but not totally out.

Frank rubbed some snow on Joe's face. Joe groaned as he waved his arms in protest.

"Sorry, buddy," Frank said. "That dart was carrying curare. It puts you to sleep and temporarily paralyzes your muscles. You'll be okay in a few minutes."

Then he went around quickly and checked the agents. They were all unconscious except for Ken Ardis, who was rubbing at his upper arm as he lay on the ground.

"I—I got hit in the arm," he said, sounding as if he'd just had a shot of novocaine.

"Can you stand?"

Ardis tried to get up but collapsed again. "Stay here," he mumbled. "Let me call the house with my radio. They'll take the chopper up."

"Call it in," Frank said. "Tell them that Joe and I are going after those guys."

Ardis shook his head. "No, stay put."

Frank ignored him. He ran to the one remaining snowmobile and pulled it up next to Joe. "Get on!"

Joe climbed on and held on tight.

Frank gunned the engine and tore off down the mountain.

"They've got a big head start," Joe shouted. His head was starting to clear.

"We'll follow their tracks in the snow," Frank

said. "We've just got to keep contact until Ardis can call in the helicopter."

Frank had the sled up to twenty miles an hour. He swerved left, just missing a tree. Low-hanging branches dumped snow on them as they flew through them.

"Where do you think they're headed?" Joe asked. He ducked down as Frank zoomed under a fallen tree trunk that had wedged itself against another tree.

"Don't know," Frank yelled. "I think I remember seeing some kind of deep ravine on the maps in Salazar's room. It was about ten or twenty miles from the lodge."

"Are we headed in that direction?"

Frank lost the tracks for a second, then swung back over to them. "Yeah. I think so."

They reached a small clearing and Joe looked up. A clear, cloudless sky, but no helicopter.

They drove back into the thick woods, bouncing over a snowdrift, then arced neatly between two trees. The snowmobile engine howled like a big-bore motorcycle.

They drove on for ten minutes or so, working hard to travel fast and stay on the tracks.

As they zipped past another tree, a big section of bark exploded, sending splinters into Joe's face. He flinched and looked back over his shoulder.

He tapped his brother on the back.

"What!"

"Somebody's tailing us," Joe yelled. "And he's not shooting darts—he's firing real bullets!"

Frank glanced back. There was another snowmobile all right, and it was gaining on them. The rider wore a dark ski mask and held an automatic pistol in one hand while he steered with the other.

"Hold on, Joe!" Frank said, zagging hard to the right.

"Don't lose the tracks," Joe warned. "We'll never find them again."

Frank yanked the wheel back to the left, almost throwing Joe off the back.

A bullet sang off a small boulder. "He's gaining on us!"

"This is no good," Frank said. "With both of us on here we're too slow. He's going to catch up at any second."

"We'll have to ditch it!" Joe shouted.

"No way!" Knowing it was almost impossible to hit a moving target while trying to control a bouncing, bucking snowmobile, Frank decided there was only one way to end this chase.

He threw the handlebars to the left and hit the hand brake. The sled went into a one-hundred-eighty-degree spin.

Now they were facing their attacker. He was only forty or fifty yards away.

Frank revved the engine and raced forward.

"Frank! Are you crazy?" Joe cried.

"Hang on!"

Like knights jousting, Frank and the other rider headed directly at each other.

Bullets ripped through the air over Joe's head. He looked past Frank's shoulder. The two sleds were only twenty yards apart now. Then fifteen, then ten, five . . .

A bullet crashed into the nose of the snowmobile, sending shards of plastic and fiberglass up at Frank.

Joe waited for Frank or the other driver to swerve.

The masked driver changed course, and not a second too soon. Joe dove at him as he passed, trying to slam a shoulder into him and knock him to the ground.

He made contact, but it wasn't solid. He rolled to a stop in the snow. Looking up, he saw the rider swerve but stay on board.

The guy hit the brakes and swung around. Again Joe was the prey. The rider bore down on him, gun blazing.

Joe lunged clear. The rider flew past. Joe expected him to spin and make a second pass, but the guy kept going and zeroed in on Frank.

They were playing chicken once more, but this was no game.

It looked to Joe as if the two sleds would merely graze each other this time. Then he saw the expression change on Frank's face. His brother steered his snowmobile right into the other rider.

Frank jumped off as the two machines slammed into each other like runaway trains. The sound echoed through the woods.

The gunman flew over his handlebars. Frank's sled rose straight into the air, then flopped down on its side and slid into a tree.

Frank was on his feet quicker than a gymnast. He sprinted toward the fallen rider. The guy appeared to be out cold.

As Frank got close he saw the gunman move. The guy rolled over and leveled his gun right at Frank's head.

"You're dead, kid!" he snarled.

15 Cliffhanger

Frank stopped in his tracks and put his hands up. He watched as the guy squeezed the trigger.

The pistol jammed—it was packed with snow.

The thug sprang to his feet just as Frank rushed him. This time Frank wasn't about to get cracked in the head. He pretended he was going in for a tackle, but then stood up straight and nailed the guy in the chest with a powerful front kick.

The gunman staggered back, still trying to get the pistol slide to work.

Frank cleverly circled to his left until his attacker's back was to Joe.

Seeing his chance, Joe slashed in and cut the guy's legs out from under him with a rolling block. The gun flew into the air, landing at Frank's feet.

He kicked it into the underbrush.

Joe was on top of the thug immediately, throwing quick punches to his ribs.

The guy rolled to one side. When Joe tried to put him in a headlock, he found himself staring at the tip of a six-inch dagger blade.

"Get off me, punk!" the man spat through the ski mask.

Joe backed away.

The thug scrambled to his feet. He jabbed the knife at each of the Hardys as they circled in close. It was obvious to Frank the man had both martial arts and weapons training.

"Stay back, Joe," he warned.

"That's right!" the man yelled, obviously trying to make his voice sound lower than it was. "Stay back or I'll gut you like a fish."

He went to his snowmobile and tried to start it. When nothing happened, he kicked it in anger.

He jogged over to the Hardys' sled and rolled it upright. It started with no problem.

The thug tucked the knife back into his ski suit and got on. "Have a nice long hike back to the house," he said. "Neal Jordan will be long gone before you get there."

He zoomed off into the woods.

"Who was that?" Joe asked. "Did one of the parachutists circle back and get behind us, or are we dealing with more than two people?"

"I don't know," Frank said. "I thought I recognized his voice for a minute, but now I can't place it."

Joe went over to the man's wrecked sled to see if he could use his mechanic's skills to get it running.

"Frank, take a look at this," he said, pointing to a small backpack strapped to the back of the snowmobile. "Our friend forgot something."

Frank unhooked the pack and opened it. "Maps," he said, pulling things out. "Maps just like the ones I saw in Salazar's room. A set of crampons, and here—two folding ice axes."

Frank tossed an ax to Joe, dumped the crampons, and stuck the other ax in the pocket of his jacket. He opened one of the maps and traced his finger along a red line.

"Looks like I was right," he said. "They're headed for this deep gorge. We're not that far from it now."

"Then I say we keep following the tracks," Joe said firmly. "There's no way I'm retreating to the house while there's still a chance we can rescue Neal."

Frank looked out into the woods. "I agree. We've got two or three hours of daylight left. Let's go."

Together they fell into a jog, staying to one side of the snowmobile tracks. They kept their eyes and ears open in case of another ambush.

A few snowflakes began to weave their way through the trees. Then, minutes later, the sprinkle turned into a heavy snowfall.

Frank picked up the pace. "We've got to hurry," he said. "This snow will cover the tracks in no time."

Around fifteen or twenty minutes later the Hardys came to the edge of a large clearing.

Frank held out his hand, motioning for Joe to stop. The brothers slowed to a walk and crept up behind a big pine with low-hanging branches.

Frank slowly pulled one branch down a little, creating a small window between two limbs. He saw a clearing that extended fifteen or twenty feet up to the edge of an enormous ravine. The rock face on the far side was nearly vertical and dropped down at least two hundred feet.

Frank waved Joe up. "We have our kidnappers," he whispered.

Joe instantly recognized all three of the men standing thirty yards or so away in the clearing. "Salazar, Sammy Fear, and . . . Ken Ardis!" he said. "Agent Ardis, man. We should've known it was an inside job." Ardis had Neal Jordan by the collar of his ski jacket.

"No wonder Ardis didn't want us watching Neal at the Max Games," Frank said. "Without us around, it would've been easy for him to set it up so Fear and Salazar could nab Neal."

"And no wonder help doesn't seem to be on the way," Joe added. "Ardis must have been faking when he said he got hit by a tranquilizer dart. He never radioed the house."

Frank nodded. "He got himself a snowmobile and came after us."

They could hear the three men talking, but couldn't make out the words.

Joe peeked through the limbs in both directions. "Where's Amanda Mollica? She definitely got on the plane with Fear and Salazar, but I don't see her."

"She might be keeping watch," Frank said. "Be careful."

Joe pointed to a pile of snow-covered branches a few yards in front of them. "There are the snowmobiles," he said. "They hid them under those branches."

The Hardys watched as Salazar dropped a climbing rope over the lip of the ravine.

Ducking down to his hands and knees, Joe crawled under the lowest branches.

"What're you doing?" Frank whispered.

Joe didn't answer. Still on his hands and knees, he stole out to the snowmobiles. Keeping one eye on the kidnappers, he gently reached under a branch and disconnected a spark plug wire on one of the sleds.

He was about to crawl around to get to another one when he saw Fear turn and walk in his direction.

He scampered back to cover next to Frank.

Fear carried one more branch over and dropped it on the snowmobiles. He checked his watch.

"We've got forty-five minutes to meet Amanda at the plane," he shouted to Ardis.

"Shut up, Sammy," Ardis yelled. "Keep working."

As Fear jogged back to the others, Frank turned to Joe. "Now we know the odds. Two of us against three of them. Mollica's not around."

The Hardys watched as Salazar, using the rope, started climbing down into the ravine.

When his head disappeared over the edge, Joe elbowed his brother in the side. "Let's rush them now," he whispered. "We can take Ardis and Fear while Salazar's on the rope."

Frank raised an eyebrow. "Wait," he said. "We don't know what's going on yet."

Joe ignored him. He burst through the branches of the tree and charged straight for Sammy Fear.

Frank had no choice but to follow. Setting his sights on Agent Ardis, he sprinted forward at full speed.

Joe drove his shoulder into Fear's thin body, slamming him to the ground. He heard the breath escape from the sky surfer's lungs.

He didn't wait for Sammy to recover. Grabbing him by the collar, Joe cracked him in the jaw with two quick jabs. Fear's body went limp.

A few yards away Frank was having a tougher time with the rogue Secret Service agent.

Ardis immediately shoved Neal aside and went into a tae kwon do stance the second he recognized

Frank. The two faced off against each other, circling slowly.

Frank stepped close and whirled into a spinning back kick.

Ardis ducked, landed a quick hook to Frank's belly, then danced clear.

Frank sucked up the pain. With a loud "Ki-yai," he faked a straight right hand. The instant he saw Ardis flinch, Frank lifted his right foot high into the air and hacked it down on Ardis's head—a perfectly executed ax kick.

Ardis dropped to one knee.

His face a grimace of rage, Neal Jordan stepped in and punched the agent in the jaw. Ardis collapsed.

"Nice shot, Neal!" a voice called. "Now get down on the ground—all of you!"

Frank looked over. Rick Salazar had climbed back up the rope and now had a pistol pointed right at Neal.

Salazar waved the gun in front of him, directing the Hardys and Neal to move away from his cohorts and lie facedown in the snow.

A couple of minutes later, he'd revived both Fear and Ardis.

"That was exciting, wasn't it," Ardis said, rubbing his jaw. He walked over to Neal and kicked him in the ribs. "I'm through baby-sitting you, kid. This time tomorrow, I'll be sitting on a beach somewhere with ten million dollars in the bank."

"My dad will catch you," Neal said bitterly. "No matter where you go."

Sammy Fear lifted Neal to his feet. "Don't count on it, dude." He shoved Neal toward the rope at the edge of the ravine. He kicked at Frank and Joe. "Get up! Get over there with him."

Salazar stuck the gun in Neal's face. "Okay. Frank, you go first." He nodded toward the rope. "There's a cave about forty feet down the face of the ravine. Climb down to it."

Keeping his eyes glued to Salazar, Frank headed down the rope. Looking up, he saw Joe and Neal being forced down after him.

Frank soon came to the cave. It was about fifteen feet wide—about the size of a one-car garage.

Frank swung onto the ledge of the cave, then helped Joe and Neal safely in.

When they'd cleared away from the rope, Salazar zipped down using a rappelling harness. He pointed the gun at Frank.

"Step back, man." He unhooked and stepped into the mouth of the cave.

Ardis rappelled down next. He stepped into the cave and shrugged off a backpack. He tossed it on the ground in front of the teens as Fear entered the cave.

"What's that?" Joe asked.

Ardis grinned. "A couple of jugs of water. One sleeping bag." He broke into a laugh. "Sorry, we thought we were going to have only one guest at our cave hotel."

They all paused. The beating sound of a helicopter approaching filled the cave.

"Those idiots at the house must've finally figured out that you're missing," he said to Neal.

"Give it up, Ardis," Frank said. "The other agents must know by now that you're behind all this."

Salazar peeked out of the cave, then turned to Ardis. "Exactly like I said, man. We're completely hidden. The only way that helicopter's going to find them is if they fly down into the ravine."

Ardis faced Frank. "They'll all think I was kidnapped along with Neal," he said. "The only person with a clue is DuBelle, and she won't have any memory of what happened once that tranquilizer wears off."

The sound of the helicopter faded into the distance.

"Go easy on that water," Ardis said as he started back up the rope. "You may be here for a very long time."

16 Over the Edge

Ardis climbed out of sight. A couple of minutes later the rope slithered out of view as one of the men pulled it up.

Joe went to the cave entrance and looked up. A small ledge projected about fifteen feet up, shielding them from view above.

"Salazar was right," Joe said glumly. "There's no way a chopper will see us."

Frank and Neal stood next to Joe and peered over the edge.

Neal picked up a pebble and chucked it. It arced out and down into the ravine. They didn't hear it hit bottom.

"It's a long way down," Neal said.

They heard the sound of snowmobiles racing away.

"They're gone," Frank said. He went over and checked the pack that Ardis had dropped. As he'd said, there was one cheap sleeping bag and some gallon jugs of water.

"How long will that last?" Neal asked.

"Not long," Frank replied. "One, two days. We'll probably freeze to death before that."

"We know the identities of the kidnappers," Joe said. "I bet Ardis isn't going to tell anyone where we are."

Neal kicked the sleeping bag. "He wants us to keep quiet permanently."

Frank nodded. "We've got to escape. Joe, you have that ice ax I gave you? I'm going to try to free climb out of here."

Joe smiled and tossed the ice ax they'd found in Ardis's pack to his brother. "I can't believe they didn't search us," he said.

Frank pulled his ax from his jacket pocket and hung it on his belt with the other one. "They were in too much of a hurry, I guess." He returned to the mouth of the cave.

"Can you make it?" Neal asked.

"I can try," Frank said. "Here, give me a boost, Joe."

Joe cupped his hands together. Frank stepped in the hand cradle and pushed himself up past the roof of the cave.

"I . . . just . . . need . . . to get past this . . . ledge," he said, concentrating hard.

Joe pushed Frank as high as he could, then watched as his brother wriggled up over the ledge and onto the sheer face of the wall. He was on his own now.

Joe turned away from the cave entrance. He didn't want to see Frank fly past if he fell.

Up on the wall, Frank stopped a second to rest. He looked down, then quickly back at the wall. That had been a mistake.

Although it was cold out, Frank was sweating. His palms were slick. Here he was, two hundred feet up without a safety line. One mistake and he was bug splatter on the rocks below.

Making sure his feet were secure on the ledge, Frank wiped the sweat from each hand on his pants.

He started climbing. Reaching up for a handhold, he edged up a foot or so. He found a small knot of rock to his right and placed his foot on it. With his left hand, he found a narrow fissure and wedged two fingers in. Even though it hurt like crazy, he pulled himself up. It felt as if the skin was being ripped from his fingers.

He made good progress; it wasn't snowing anymore—that was a good thing. When he hit a patch of ice or a slippery spot, he would pull one of the ice axes from his belt and find a secure place to hammer it in.

Nearing the top, he jammed the toe of his boot into a crack. He tugged on the ice ax over his head. It seemed tight.

He took a deep breath and pushed.

It was as though someone had kicked a step ladder out from under him. The support disappeared from under his foot and Frank flopped against the wall. He hung on for dear life, supported only by the two ax handles.

He looked down in time to see the rock fall away, ricochet off the wall, then tumble into space.

Inside the cave, Neal let out a frightened shout.

"Frank!" Joe yelled, spinning to face the mouth of the cave. He looked at Neal. "What did you see?"

"Just a rock," Neal said. "A rock flew past. For a second I thought it was Frank. Sorry, man."

Joe didn't reply. He stared down at his clenched fists.

Frank scrambled to find a foothold. He didn't know how long the axes would stay secure. His left boot caught on something firm. He looked down. A gnarled root grew out of the rock face.

Frank clawed his way up, finally reaching the top. He tossed the ice axes aside and surveyed the clearing. For a minute he thought he'd have to leave Joe and Neal while he went for help, but then he spotted Salazar's coil of rope next to the trunk of a tree.

Making sure the rope was secure, Frank tossed it over the side. "Come on up!"

He helped Neal up first. As they were waiting for Joe to reach the top, they heard the helicopter approaching.

Frank offered Joe a hand, and the chopper broke over the clearing, blades thumping.

Neal waved wildly. "Down here! Down here!"

Frank smiled. "They see us," he said.

The pilot set the big chopper down at a wide spot in the clearing about fifty yards away. The three teens ran to meet it.

They ducked under the pounding blades, the downdraft whipping at their hair.

Agent DuBelle slid the side door open and helped Neal aboard. "Get on!" she yelled.

Joe shook his head. "It was Salazar, Fear, and Agent Ardis!" he shouted. "They got away on snowmobiles."

DuBelle's eyes narrowed in anger. "Agent Ardis was involved?"

Neal nodded.

"Amanda Mollica's waiting for them somewhere nearby with their plane," Frank said. "Find her. Joe and I are going after Ardis."

DuBelle started to protest, but the Hardys weren't listening. They both sprinted for the snowmobile Joe had disabled earlier.

"The tracks lead south," Frank said, taking one of the maps from his pocket.

The chopper took off as Joe reconnected the spark plug wire and fired the sled to life.

"Here!" Frank said, pointing to a red mark on the map. "Here's a flat area long enough to land a small plane. That's where they're going."

He and Frank jumped on and rocketed after the kidnappers.

Joe stayed away from the trees. "I figure they're traveling through the woods," he said. "They don't want to be spotted from the air."

"Right!" Frank shouted. "We'll make better time if we stay in the clearing."

Joe hugged the edge of the ravine. They roared along, and sooner than they expected, Frank caught a glimpse of a snowmobile through the trees.

"Just ahead!" he shouted. "We're right on top of them."

Fear and Salazar were on one sled, while Ardis drove the other. Joe saw Salazar point back at them.

"They've seen us!"

The two fleeing snowmobiles darted out into the clearing so they could go faster.

Joe opened the throttle and surged ahead.

A cone of flame flashed from Salazar's gun as he squeezed off three rounds in quick succession.

Fearlessly, Joe pulled up right behind them. Counting on Frank to take the wheel, he jumped.

This time Joe connected perfectly with his target. He knocked both Salazar and Fear off their sled, and the three of them tumbled and somer-saulted in the snow.

When Joe jumped, Frank grabbed the handle-bars and steered toward Agent Ardis.

Joe struggled to his feet. Salazar lay a few feet away, unconscious. The butt of his gun stuck out of a snowbank.

Joe turned to face Sammy Fear, who stood close to the edge of the ravine. Joe rushed Fear, confi-dent he could take the skinny punk with no problem.

He grabbed Fear by his jumpsuit and tried to wrestle him to the ground. But Sammy was agile, and he managed to get free.

Joe went after him again, expecting him to run.

Fear didn't run. He jumped. He jumped, disap-pearing over the lip of the ravine.

Joe stopped in shock. "No way!"

Then he realized what Fear had done. He ran over to Salazar and ripped the pack off his back. Just as he had thought—a small BASE-jumping chute.

Joe strapped it on, then pitched himself over the side and into the ravine.

Meanwhile, Frank had caught up to Ardis. He dove from his sled, knocking Ardis into a thick snowdrift. The two snowmobiles plowed over the edge of the cliff.

This time Frank knew the agent's weakness. He faked a side kick, then threw a spinning back fist.

His knuckles caught Ardis flush in the face. The agent crumpled in the snow, blood dripping from his broken nose.

Frank found Ardis's radio and called for help.

Joe plummeted into the ravine headfirst. Rocks that had seemed so far away, suddenly appeared to be rushing up at him at super speed.

Fear had a head start. Joe knew the only way to catch up to him was to let himself free-fall farther than Fear. That way he'd get to the bottom first.

He waited. He kept waiting.

Mere seconds before impact, Joe tossed the chute away. It opened with a powerful snap. The harness dug into his armpits as he slowed.

He slammed into the ground right next to Sammy Fear.

Fear tried to run before releasing his chute. Joe watched him get tangled in the cords and trip.

Joe laughed as he cut his own chute free and walked over to Fear.

"Sammy," he said. "You look like a bug caught in a web."

The next afternoon the Hardys and Jamal stood on the steps of the Bayport courthouse waiting for the president of the United States to pin medals of bravery on their chests.

"So," Jamal whispered to Joe. "What do you think made Ardis do it?"

"Greed," Joe said. "And Salazar and Fear got involved for the money and the thrill, I think."

"They claim they had no idea Ardis planned to let Neal die in the cave," Frank added. "But kidnapping the president's son—that's still very serious."

"They were serious about putting us out of commission when they attacked us at the van," Joe said. "Rick tried to dump Frank off the ice wall, and Sammy admitted he messed with my parachute. Those two are going away for a long time."

"Mollica says she had no idea what was going on," Frank whispered. "The FBI's still evaluating her statements."

Two Secret Service agents came out of the front door of the courthouse, followed by the president.

After a short speech, he lifted three medals from a satin case and turned to face the three teens.

"I thank you," the president said as he pinned a medal to Frank's suitcoat. "And my son thanks you."

The president finished and stepped aside. Neal came up and knocked fists with the three friends. "So, you fellas are gonna spend the rest of the winter break snowboarding at the lodge, right?"

"Absolutely," Jamal said.

Neal smiled. "Cool."

When Neal went back to stand next to his dad, a crush of reporters surrounded the Hardys and Jamal.

"Frank! Joe! Jamal!" A familiar voice shouted. "Can I use you guys in my advertisements for next year's Max Games?"

It was Fred Vale.

Joe smiled at the camera. "No way, Vale. I think we're maxed out on the Max Games for a while."

THE HARDY BOYS® SERIES By Franklin W. Dixon

LOOK FOR AN EXCITING NEW
HARDY BOYS MYSTERY COMING FROM
MINSTREL® BOOKS

NANCY DREW® MYSTERY STORIES By Carolyn Keene

☐	#58: THE FLYING SAUCER MYSTERY	72320-0/$3.99	☐	#114: THE SEARCH FOR THE SILVER PERSIAN	79300-4/$3.99
☐	#62: THE KACHINA DOLL MYSTERY	67220-7/$3.99	☐	#115: THE SUSPECT IN THE SMOKE	79301-2/$3.99
☐	#68: THE ELUSIVE HEIRESS	62478-4/$3.99	☐	#116: THE CASE OF THE TWIN TEDDY BEARS	79302-0/$3.99
☐	#72: THE HAUNTED CAROUSEL	66227-9/$3.99	☐	#117: MYSTERY ON THE MENU	79303-9/$3.99
☐	#73: ENEMY MATCH	64283-9/$3.50	☐	#118: TROUBLE AT LAKE TAHOE	79304-7/$3.99
☐	#77: THE BLUEBEARD ROOM	66857-9/$3.50	☐	#119: THE MYSTERY OF THE MISSING MASCOT	87202-8/$3.99
☐	#79: THE DOUBLE HORROR OF FENLEY PLACE	64387-8/$3.99	☐	#120: THE CASE OF THE FLOATING CRIME	87203-6/$3.99
☐	#81: MARDI GRAS MYSTERY	64961-2/$3.99	☐	#121: THE FORTUNE-TELLER'S SECRET	87204-4/$3.99
☐	#83: THE CASE OF THE VANISHING VEIL	63413-5/$3.99	☐	#122: THE MESSAGE IN THE HAUNTED MANSION	87205-2/$3.99
☐	#84: THE JOKER'S REVENGE	63414-3/$3.99	☐	#123: THE CLUE ON THE SILVER SCREEN	87206-0/$3.99
☐	#85: THE SECRET OF SHADY GLEN	63416-X/$3.99	☐	#124: THE SECRET OF THE SCARLET HAND	87207-9/$3.99
☐	#87: THE CASE OF THE RISING STAR	66312-7/$3.99	☐	#125: THE TEEN MODEL MYSTERY	87208-7/$3.99
☐	#89: THE CASE OF THE DISAPPEARING DEEJAY	66314-3/$3.99	☐	#126: THE RIDDLE IN THE RARE BOOK	87209-5/$3.99
☐	#91: THE GIRL WHO COULDN'T REMEMBER	66316-X/$3.99	☐	#127: THE CASE OF THE DANGEROUS SOLUTION	50500-9/$3.99
☐	#92: THE GHOST OF CRAVEN COVE	66317-8/$3.99	☐	#128: THE TREASURE IN THE ROYAL TOWER	50502-5/$3.99
☐	#93: THE CASE OF THE SAFECRACKER'S SECRET	66318-6/$3.99	☐	#129: THE BABYSITTER BURGLARIES	50507-6/$3.99
☐	#94: THE PICTURE-PERFECT MYSTERY	66319-4/$3.99	☐	#130: THE SIGN OF THE FALCON	50508-4/$3.99
☐	#96: THE CASE OF THE PHOTO FINISH	69281-X/$3.99	☐	#131: THE HIDDEN INHERITANCE	50509-2/$3.99
☐	#97: THE MYSTERY AT MAGNOLIA MANSION	69282-8/$3.99	☐	#132: THE FOX HUNT MYSTERY	50510-6/$3.99
☐	#98: THE HAUNTING OF HORSE ISLAND	69284-4/$3.99	☐	#133: THE MYSTERY AT THE CRYSTAL PALACE	50515-7/$3.99
☐	#99: THE SECRET AT SEVEN ROCKS	69285-2/$3.99	☐	#134: THE SECRET OF THE FORGOTTEN CAVE	50516-5/$3.99
☐	#101: THE MYSTERY OF THE MISSING MILLIONAIRES	69287-9/$3.99	☐	#135: THE RIDDLE OF THE RUBY GAZELLE	00048-9/$3.99
☐	#102: THE SECRET IN THE DARK	69279-8/$3.99	☐	#136: THE WEDDING DAY MYSTERY	00050-0/$3.99
☐	#104: THE MYSTERY OF THE JADE TIGER	73050-9/$3.99	☐	#137: IN SEARCH OF THE BLACK ROSE	00051-9/$3.99
☐	#107: THE LEGEND OF MINER'S CREEK	73053-3/$3.99	☐	#138: THE LEGEND OF THE LOST GOLD	00049-7/$3.99
☐	#109: THE MYSTERY OF THE MASKED RIDER	73055-X/$3.99	☐	NANCY DREW GHOST STORIES	69132-5/$3.99
☐	#110: THE NUTCRACKER BALLET MYSTERY	73056-8/$3.99	☐	#139: THE SECRET OF CANDLELIGHT INN	00052-7/$3.99
☐	#111: THE SECRET AT SOLAIRE	79297-0/$3.99	☐	#140: THE DOOR-TO-DOOR DECEPTION	00053-5/$3.99
☐	#112: CRIME IN THE QUEEN'S COURT	79298-9/$3.99	☐	#141: THE WILD CAT CRIME	00120-5/$3.99
☐	#113: THE SECRET LOST AT SEA	79299-7/$3.99	☐	#142: THE CASE OF CAPTIAL INTRIGUE	00751-3/$3.99

A MINSTREL® BOOK

Published by Pocket Books

Simon & Schuster, Mail Order Dept. HB5, 200 Old Tappan Rd., Old Tappan, N.J. 07675
Please send me copies of the books checked. Please add appropriate local sales tax.
☐ Enclosed full amount per copy with this coupon (Send check or money order only)
☐ If order is $10.00 or more, you may charge to one of the following accounts: ☐ Mastercard   ☐ Visa
Please be sure to include proper postage and handling: 0.95 for first copy; 0.50 for each additional copy ordered.

Name _____

Address _____

City _____   State/Zip _____

Credit Card # _____   Exp.Date _____

Signature _____

Books listed are also available at your bookstore. Prices are subject to change without notice.

760-29